THE BLACK

Simon felt as if he was seeing the mountain properly for the first time. Halfway up the wild slope, just where the purple blended into the brown and green, shone a bright blue light . . . as bright as a star at midnight. As he gazed at it the horn began to move in his hands. He held it lightly, and let it twist . . . He felt beads of sweat standing out on his forehead. His back was suddenly icy cold. He shivered.

Simon cannot resist being drawn into danger and enchantment, but he has little idea of the challenges he's about to face.

'. . . a good blend of realism and fantasy, simply but excitingly told.'

The Guardian

The Black Horn

Clare Cooper

Illustrated by
Trevor Stubley

KNIGHT BOOKS
Hodder and Stoughton

Text copyright © Clare Cooper 1981
Illustrations copyright © Hodder & Stoughton Ltd 1981

First published by Hodder & Stoughton Children's Books 1981

Knight Books edition 1984
Second impression 1985

British Library C.I.P.

Cooper, Clare
    The Black Horn.
    I. Title
    823'.914[J]   PZ7

    ISBN 0-340-34851-8

Printed and bound in Great Britain for Hodder and
Stoughton Paperbacks, a division of Hodder and
Stoughton Ltd., Mill Road, Dunton Green, Sevenoaks,
Kent (Editorial Office: 47 Bedford Square, London,
WC1 3DP) by Cox & Wyman Ltd., Reading.

Contents

I An Encounter with Billy Bowcett

'Why don't you go down and ask?' Mother suggested. Simon shook his head.

'No, they don't really want anybody else on board,' he said, 'and, anyway, I don't really want to crew for Mr Bowcett.'

'Oh, Simon!' Mother looked exasperated. 'What are you going to do, then? You can come with us if you like, you know, but it will be dreadfully boring hanging about, waiting, all day.'

'Don't worry,' he said. 'There's plenty to do. I'll find something.'

His father came in from the garden, where he had been sitting quietly in the sun with his eyes shut. Simon had seen him there. He looked worse with his eyes shut. He looked ill enough with them open. His eyes were so big and dark now, since his illness. The look in them frightened Simon sometimes. But with them shut, all you could see was a thin, white face which didn't look like Dad at all.

'What's the matter, Dil?' he asked.

'Nothing, love, nothing.' Simon knew that his father mustn't be worried.

'She's a bit bothered because I might not have enough to do. But there's no need to worry, really. There's heaps to do here. I'll find something. I just

7

don't fancy sailing,' he explained. His father nodded, and suddenly grinned. It was the first time Simon had seen him smile for months.

'Women!' he said. 'As if a boy couldn't find something to do in a place like this, with the beach and the mountain . . . especially the mountain.'

Simon agreed with him . . . 'especially the mountain'. It was wonderful, more wonderful than any other place he had even seen, and here he was, living on it. It felt much more like home, already, than Petts Wood had ever felt. He felt as though he belonged here. He wished that he had been born here, in this village at the foot of the mountain, so that he could have lived here all his life. Last week he had been determined that he would stay here for ever. But now, Billy Bowcett had arrived, and he wasn't so sure about it any more.

Dad was still smiling when he climbed into the car, and Mother looked happier, too, as she waved goodbye and drove off down the narrow, over-grown lane which led from the cottage to the main Carmarthen road. Simon watched them go, then carefully locked the back door and hid the key in its special hole under the middle stone at the back of the rockery. He disturbed a large family of wood-lice, and watched them as they scurried away in all directions. He poked one large one, gently, and it obligingly rolled up into a neat, iron-plated ball. He liked to see them do that. They looked like shiny, grey seeds.

'If they were seeds, what would they grow into?' he wondered as he dawdled along the lane looking for more insects in the hedges.

He liked insects. They were easy to see with his sort of eyes. He would have liked to watch birds, too, but he was too shortsighted to see them properly. He needed to get close to things to be able to study them. There were bees everywhere today, all over the pink blossom on the brambles; and the buddleia bush on the corner, where the lane opened out into the church car park, was covered with butterflies. He counted five tortoise-shells, two red admirals and one peacock without even trying to see them all.

The car park was full of shoppers' cars. The village had been half empty last week, but now that the schools had broken up, it was suddenly over-flowing with people and traffic, especially in the mornings, when everybody stocked up. They all rushed out to the beach in the afternoons. He decided that he would go to the beach during the morning, then leave it when the crowd arrived. He might avoid Billy Bowcett that way.

'Why did he have to come here for his holidays?' he thought, and kicked a stone, hard, into the hedge. 'Of all the places that he could go to every year, he has to choose the place we come to live in. I'm never going to get rid of him!' He peered at the blur of faces in the crowded high street. 'Maybe he won't see me in this mob,' he thought. 'The trouble is, I'll never see him until it's too late to dodge him. He's sure to see me first.'

He was right. Billy Bowcett did see him first, but he pretended not to. He was carrying a pair of long, newly-varnished oars over his broad shoulder as he marched briskly down the middle of the pave-

9

ment. The crowd made way. He ignored Simon, who had stepped aside to the edge of the high kerb, when he realised what was coming. Then, just as he passed him, Billy twisted slightly, so that the flat blades of the oars swung sharply. Simon saw them coming, just too late. He turned away, and ducked, but not quickly enough. The edge of one blade caught him smartly on the back of his head, and he fell off the kerb into the gutter.

He knew exactly what Billy Bowcett would say. 'Oh, Jonesy, Jonesy, Jonesy! Can't you see where you're going! Poor old four eyes, in the way again!' Hardly one day passed at school without him hearing those words. Billy's usual trick was a foot stuck out to trip him as he passed, or a barge from his hard, muscular shoulder to send him reeling against the equally hard wall.

He picked himself up with the words ringing in his ears, and adjusted his glasses which had slipped forward to the end of his nose. He could feel his eyes beginning to fill with tears. His right knee and both of his hands were grazed and stinging badly. He was determined not to cry, and blinked and glared furiously at a thin girl, in a tight, yellow-and-black, striped dress, who was staring at him from across the road.

She didn't seem to be at all interested, she just stood there, staring blankly. But, as Billy walked away, laughing loudly, Simon was sure he saw her signal to an old, white dog which was sitting at her feet. It wasn't much of a signal, just a snap of her fingers and a quick point towards Billy. The old dog heaved itself to its feet, and shambled, panting

horribly, across the road. It jumped up on to the
pavement with surprising agility, and deliberately
walked straight in front of the boy.

Billy tripped, trod on the dog, and stumbled

forward with the oars swinging wildly. The dog began to make a terrible noise. It yelped and whined and howled all at the same time, while Billy, unable to save himself, fell against a parked car. He jerked the oars up, just in time, to avoid the windscreen, but they made a terrible, graunching clatter as they scraped along the roof.

'You clumsy oaf!' The owner of the car came rushing out of the supermarket and grabbed Billy by the collar. Several old ladies clustered around the dog, and began making a fuss about it all. The dog kept up the hideous din, sitting in the middle of the pavement with its nose pointing to the sky.

Simon turned and glanced at the girl. He had expected her to rush forward to comfort her dog, but she hadn't moved. She was standing in exactly the same place, with a look of glee on her face. She wasn't at all worried about the dog, she didn't even seem to notice him. It was Billy she was laughing at. She was absolutely delighted to see him in trouble.

2 *Ty Corn Du*

Simon thought about the girl as he kicked his way across the soft sand beside the river. She looked just like a hover-fly in that striped dress, all long and thin, a sort of flattened-sideways thinness.

'I wonder why she doesn't like Billy?' he thought. 'I wonder if he's bullied her, or perhaps she's got a younger brother.'

Billy wasn't going to enjoy his sailing today. His dad had been even more furious than the man who owned the car. He had come rushing up, purple in the face and red all over his shiny bald head. He had tried to pacify the man. Simon had watched him trying to laugh it off, with his gold fillings flashing in the sunlight, but he hadn't been smiling when he agreed to pay for the damage.

'It almost makes you feel sorry for Billy,' he thought as he turned to watch the sailing boats heading for the open sea. 'It might be nice to sail,' he thought. 'But only with someone you liked. Steering must be quite tricky, especially when you're tacking or racing. It would be interesting to work out exactly how far you could lean over without tipping up.' He shaded his eyes and squinted at the boats in the bay. The ones in the distance were just moving blobs of red and blue, with here and there a flash of gleaming white, but, closer to the shore, the sails were like narrow lines making a sharp angle with the deep blue sea as they raced towards him. He liked these brightly-coloured angles. 'You could work out the different angles,' he thought, 'and you would have to work out the wind speed too, I expect. Sailing must be fun.' Dad had been good at things like sailing. 'Maybe when Dad's better . . .' He didn't like to think about that.

A broad, shallow river flowed slowly, in a big, wide loop, across the sands towards the sea. He had waded through one side of the loop, where it bordered the old, stone quay and the sailing beach. Now he trotted across the hard sand towards the other side, which meandered beside the sand dunes and the top of the beach. He suddenly wanted to run fast, and sped across the open space as far as he could before his breath ran out. It wasn't far. Then he dawdled along, picking up birds' feathers.

There were hundreds of them there. Long, strong, grey ones with black pointed tips, grey ones with white down around the quill end, and long, thin, brown-and-white striped ones. There were small, soft brown-and-white ones, too, and he supposed they must come from the same kind of bird. He sat down and spread them all out in front of him, sorting them into groups of the same kind.

'Someone ought to write a book on how to identify birds from the feathers you find,' he said to himself. 'Then people like me who don't see very well could be bird watchers too.'

'A lot of bird books *do* do that,' said a bossy-sounding voice somewhere over his head. He jumped, startled, and scrambled to his feet. It was the hover-fly girl. She was sitting astride a white donkey with black ears and black hooves and sad, black eyes. The old, white dog was standing beside her, still panting horribly. 'A lot of bird books *do* do that,' she repeated. 'They also give details of songs and calls. You're not deaf as well as short-sighted, are you?' He shook his head. 'Well then you too can be a bird watcher.'

'Thank you,' he said. It sounded silly, but it had seemed the only thing to say. She made him feel that he should be grateful for the information.

She sat quite still on the angular, white back and stared down at him. She still didn't look interested, and Simon wondered why she didn't ride on past him. The donkey hung its head and shut its eyes, dozing on its feet. The dog sat down and began to scratch itself furiously behind its left ear. It shut its eyes and grinned with ecstasy.

'Is he all right now?' Simon asked, crouching to watch him closely.

'He wasn't hurt,' the girl said. 'It's a trick.' Simon stared at the dog, he certainly didn't seem to be in pain. 'I wouldn't go too close, if I was you,' she said. 'He's lousy, and they tend to "abandon ship" when he scratches.'

'You mean, he's got fleas?' Simon asked.

'Yes, a vast army of them, and a tick or two, I expect.'

'It must be a good place for fleas, in there.' Simon was interested in fleas. He had never seen

15

one, but he had read a lot about them. He looked at the thick, matted hair. 'It's nearly as long as a sheep's fleece, isn't it.'

'Longer!' she said. 'He's quite thin inside it all.'

'Why don't you cut it? He looks hot.'

'Protection,' she said, simply, and he thought of Billy's big foot as he trod down heavily.

'A cushion effect,' he said.

'Exactly.'

He stood up and looked at the girl again.

'Don't you like Billy Bowcett?' he asked.

'I've nothing against him personally. It's the company he keeps that I detest,' she said, kicking the donkey which lurched forward and began walking even before it opened its eyes.

Simon watched her ride away with the dog close to the donkey's heels. He sorted through his feathers again, then left them, and followed the hoof marks to the river. The dog was sitting whining softly to himself on a patch of dry sand. He seemed to have been left in charge of her sandals. The donkey was standing, fast asleep again, up to its knees in water, and the girl was wading steadily through the shallows, with her back bent and her face so close to the surface that the ends of her straight, black hair dipped right in.

'Can you see fish?' she asked, without looking up.

'I've never tried,' Simon said.

She stood up and stared at him.

'You're a bit of a towny, aren't you!' she said critically.

'What's wrong with that?' Simon was beginning

to think he didn't really care for the way she spoke to him.

'Nothing, in town,' she said, quite reasonably, 'but it means you miss an awful lot when you're in the country, doesn't it?' He had to agree. 'Come on in and look for flat fish,' she said. 'Take off your daps, then you can feel them under your toes, even if you can't see them clearly.'

Simon could see them. Small, brown plates in a flurry of sand, which sped across the river bed before disappearing again as they landed and lay still and blended with the mottled brown and gold, perfectly camouflaged. There were other fish too, with big, blunt heads, tapering tails and fins like delicately spread fans. But he liked the shrimps best. They appeared from nowhere, and clustered around his toes every time he stood still. They tickled unbearably after a while, as they stroked and prodded with their tiny claws, and swam over his feet with rapidly-waving legs.

Simon hadn't enjoyed a morning so much for a long time. He and the hover-fly girl waded down stream, talking and laughing, then turned and waded back up to the dog, whose whining had become slightly frantic as they walked further and further away, but calmed down to a low moan or two as they came near again. Then they waded up stream, and back again when the dog began to yelp. The donkey slept through it all. Its hooves and legs were bristling with shrimps each time they passed it.

At last, the girl said that she must go home. She sat beside the dog and began to pull on her sandals.

'It must be lunch time,' she said, 'judging by the Oysters.'

'Oysters! Are there oysters here too?' Simon asked, as he sat beside her and began to pull on his sand-shoes.

'No, not real ones. I mean the people.' She pointed to a row of cars parked beside the sand dunes. 'You know, it's from "Alice". "And thick and fast they came at last, and more and more and more." My friend Mr Smith thought of it.'

Simon nodded thoughtfully. 'It's a good name. There does seem to be an awful lot of them suddenly.'

'Yes! An awful lot of awful people! I don't like them at all, but Mr Smith says they all bring their "pearls" with them, and people like him in business out here could do with all the profit.'

Simon thought that Mr Smith sounded interesting. 'Does Mr Smith live in the village?' he asked.

The girl didn't answer. She had shaded her eyes with her hands, and was peering at a small, motor dinghy which was speeding rapidly towards them from the sailing beach. Simon could vaguely see that there was more than one person in it.

'Bother! It's Pettigrew and your friend Bowcett,' she said. Simon thought that she looked just a little frightened. 'I must get across the river before they arrive, or they'll take great delight in swamping me with their wash. Gwenhwyfar!' she called to the donkey, who lurched awake and trotted obediently towards her. She tucked up her dress and scrambled on to its back, calling the dog with a piercing whistle. It shot to her side and leapt into the water with a sharp yelp of discomfort and distaste.

As they disappeared into the dunes, Simon suddenly felt very alone. He cast one quick glance at the rapidly approaching dinghy, and took a brief look at the vast expanse of sand between him and the safety of the mountain. He knew all about Billy Bowcett's methods of getting his own back. If he saw him there he would take the chance of 'getting' him while he could. Pettigrew, whoever he was, might even help. The girl was afraid of him. He was probably just as nasty as Billy.

He made up his mind quickly, and ran for the dunes. The river was shallow at first. He splashed through at top speed. Then it deepened suddenly. He stumbled and fell forward up to his waist. He couldn't run there. He waded, breathlessly, his heart pounding, then splashed through the shallows on the far side, and staggered across the narrow beach to the path the hover-fly girl had taken. He didn't dare look at the dinghy. He could hear it. It was very close.

The path curved sharply to the left. He knew he couldn't run any more. Perhaps he would be safe there. He would hide. He crawled up a steep, sandy bank between thick bushes of marram grass, and fell into a shallow hollow at the top. He lay still, gasping for breath, listening for the sound of the motor. He couldn't hear it. It had stopped!

'Yahoo!' Billy was on to him already. He leapt from the top of the bank like an Apache silhouetted against the blue sky. Simon squirmed aside just in time. Billy landed heavily beside him. He stretched out one big hand and grabbed him by the shirt. 'Got you, Jonesy!' Simon shut his eyes and waited for the punch.

Suddenly a terrible commotion filled the hollow. He opened his eyes again. A round, white ball of snarling, snapping dog had launched itself into a frantic gallop around them. There was sand everywhere. Billy shouted and let go. He leapt to his feet, aiming a kick at the dog. It dodged smartly, yelping loudly at the same time, then darted in to collide with his legs as it had that morning. Simon scrambled out of the hollow as the big boy crashed to the ground.

'Over here!' The hover-fly girl was waiting on the path. 'You'd better ride,' she said, and half pushed him up on to the donkey's back. 'Bedwyr will keep him busy while we get away. Pettigrew stayed in the boat, thank heavens. Hup, Gwen!' She slapped the donkey smartly, and Simon hung on grimly as they jolted rapidly along the sandy path.

She whistled the dog when they reached the safety of the busy, open golf course, but still kept the donkey at a smart trot.

'Grip with your knees,' she shouted at Simon. 'You'll bounce off in a minute if you don't.' He tried hard, but his leg muscles were weak. He noticed with envy that she wasn't even out of breath although she had been running slightly uphill for at least half a mile.

They stopped at the beach car park, and she turned to look back.

'Good! They didn't chase us. I didn't expect Bowcett to, but you never know how far Pettigrew will go if he doesn't get his own way. He's horrible! Did you hear him laughing when Billy jumped you?'

Simon shook his head. 'I only heard Billy and your dog.'

'Yes! Good old Bedwyr!' She bent and scratched his back, making him wriggle and writhe with delight. 'You could do with a dog like him to take care of you.'

She stood up and looked at him critically again. 'Well, I can't leave you here, and I can't send you back at their mercy. Pettigrew would have a lovely time with you! It might be a good idea if you came to lunch with us. They'll have cleared off by this afternoon, they practise for the regatta every day until tea time. You can phone your family from our house to stop them worrying.'

'Actually, there's no-one home, so I won't be missed until tea time,' he said. He was very glad not to have to face that long, lonely walk, with Billy possibly lying in wait.

'Right then. Off you get! I'll ride the rest of the way. The Oysters tear down this road to the beach, Gwenhwyfar can't stand them, she'll need a bit of persuasion.'

They set off along the narrow road through the golf course and up over the hill, past fields full of black and white cows. Luckily, only a few cars passed them and most of them slowed down carefully, for Gwenhwyfar certainly didn't like them at all. She stood, stiff and absolutely still, every time one drove near, and gradually leaned over sideways into the hedge, until the hover-fly seemed perilously near being tipped off. Bedwyr didn't like them either. He tried to wrap himself around Simon's legs every time he saw one.

They didn't talk at all until they reached a narrow gateway at the end of a shady avenue of tall beech trees. It all looked very uncared-for. The gate posts were rounded pillars of flat, grey slates stuck together with crumbling mortar. Small ferns and pennywort grew in every crack, and a low bush of fumitory, like pink smoke, nestled at the base of one, while the ditch on the other side was full of tall, red campions. Stinging nettles and dock grew up through the rusty gate, where it lay, just inside the drive, and the drive itself looked as though it hadn't been weeded for an age. There were two tyre marks on either side, but the middle was a long, narrow strip of tall, wheat-like grasses and red poppies.

Simon thought that he had never seen anywhere so beautiful. It felt safe, too, as safe as the mountain. He looked up through the leaves of the silver-trunked trees, and gazed at the ever-moving blur of green and blue and golden sunlight. He suddenly felt relaxed and happy.

'This is a very special place,' he told himself. 'It's just as special as the mountain.'

'Welcome to Ty Corn Du,' the girl said.

'Ty Corn Du! Our cottage is called something like that.' Simon wasn't really surprised that the two places should have the same name. It seemed right somehow.

'You're never the people in Ty Corn Du Fach?' The girl was surprised. 'Well, what a coincidence! It used to belong to my family, oh, years and years ago.'

'What do the names mean?'

'House of the black horn, and little house of the black horn, roughly.'

'Why, "black horn"?'

'I'll show you when we get there.'

Ty Corn Du was just as beautiful as the avenue, in its own way, in spite of its broken windows and holes in the roof. The garden was completely wild and full of brilliant colour. There seemed to be rhododendrons everywhere. Some of them were so big that they almost hid the grey stone walls of the house. Their flowers were full of bumble bees.

'What's your name, apart from Jonesy?' the girl asked as she turned Gwenhwyfar loose in a small, stone-walled paddock full of lush grass and tall, white daisies.

'Simon,' he said. 'What's yours?'

'Ah . . . Iseulte,' she said.

'She made that up!' he thought. 'Why did she do that?'

She threw open the big white door, and he saw at once why the house was called Corn Du. There, straight in front of him, mounted on a shield of dark wood, was a long, twisted, black horn.

As soon as Simon saw it he knew that it was no ordinary horn. He knew, somehow, that this was the horn of a Unicorn.

3　*The Horn*

Simon held the horn in his hands as he watched the hover-fly girl beat up eggs for an omelette. He turned it as he ran his finger along the smooth, perfect spiral, from the pointed tip to the broad base. There was a hollow place there, round and polished. He picked up half an egg shell and pushed it into the hole. It fitted easily.

'That's where the carbuncle is supposed to be hidden,' the girl said. 'Pettigrew told us all about it. We didn't even know it would unscrew from the wall, but he had it down and was looking for the wretched thing as soon as he walked through the front door. He knows all about how to make money without actually doing any work, does Pettigrew.'

'I thought he was your enemy.'

'Oh he is! But we didn't know it then. My father brought him home, him and Mr Smith. They were all at college at the same time, and met up again one day, a couple of years ago, at some Economists' Conference in Cardiff. Anyway, Father brought them home. Mr Smith was wonderful, but Pettigrew . . . Do you know what he did? He came back the very next day and tried to buy the house from Meryl! She's my aunt, by the way. Well! Imagine Pettigrew owning Ty Corn Du!'

'She couldn't sell it to him. Not if he's like Billy Bowcett.' Simon was horrified at the idea.

'Well, he is like Bowcett, really, but he pretends not to be which makes him much, much worse. Meryl loathes him. She wouldn't dream of selling the place to anyone, but especially not to any one like Pettigrew.'

'I suppose he was mad when she said no.'

'Furious! He went bright red, then ghastly white, just like that!' She snapped her fingers. 'He couldn't speak, he was so angry. He stalked out without saying another word. But do you know what he did a few days later . . . he came back with red roses for her. As if she needed them, with a garden bursting at the seams with flowers! And, oh, did he ladle on the charm! It oozed out of him from every greasy pore. He's still at it now. *I* think he's trying to get her to marry him. You know, if he can't get Ty Corn Du by fair means, he'll get it by foul.' She gave the eggs another furious beating. 'She won't marry *him* though. I think she dreads the very thought of his visitations.'

'But why does Pettigrew want the place so badly?' Simon asked.

'Oh, he says he wants to convert it into holiday flats. It might be the real reason. He says he could make a fortune out of it. He's always thinking about money. He wouldn't understand about loving the house. It was the same with the horn. All he thought about was the carbuncle.'

'What's a carbuncle got to do with money?'

'Oh, a carbuncle is an old name for a ruby,' she explained. 'A Unicorn is supposed to have one hidden at the base of its horn.'

'It must be a huge one,' Simon said, thinking

about the egg shell.

'Absolutely! But it's all a lot of codswallop, of course. That's a narwhal's tusk, really.'

'No! It's not! It's a Unicorn's horn. It is, you know. I'm sure it is.'

She looked at him strangely. 'Don't be daft!' He blushed scarlet, and said nothing. He couldn't explain to her how the horn felt in his hands. It was warm, almost throbbing with a life of its own. No cold, fish-like creature would produce a thing like this. It came from a Unicorn, he was sure, a warm gentle, perfect Unicorn.

She was still looking at him strangely.

'Pettigrew was sure it was a real Unicorn's horn,' she said. 'He fancies himself as a bit of a dyn hysbys, that's a kind of wizard,' she explained. 'Just because his grandad came from Myddfai! But, I ask you, who could be a wizard with a name like Pettigrew!'

'What's special about Myddfai?' Simon asked. 'My granny came from there.'

Now she really stared at him strangely. She looked from his face to the black horn, and then back to his face again. He thought that she was going to say something rude about his ignorance, but she didn't. She gave the eggs yet another thorough beating, then, as she cooked the omelette, she told him the story of the Physicians of Myddfai. Of the farmer's fairy wife who left him because he had hit her three times, and went back to her own people in the magic lake Llyn y Fan Fawr, taking all her fairy cattle with her, but leaving her knowledge of healing and other mysteries to her sons, who became the first Physicians of Myddfai.

'So you see, Pettigrew believes that he might have a little fairy blood in his veins, or magic in his bones, or something, just because his grandfather came from there,' she said. 'You don't fancy yourself as a bit of a wizard, I suppose?'

'Oh no! I'm going to be a mathematician when I grow up.'

'How dull!'

Simon flushed again. 'Well, I could be an expert on insects, or a chess player.'

'That's more interesting. A famous chess player.

Yes, I like that idea. Mr Smith plays chess. He's rather good at it. Do you know what I'm going to be?' Simon thought that she would make a good school mistress, but he didn't say so. On second thoughts, he decided that she might think this rather dull.

'What?' he asked.

She pulled her long hair loose from where she had it tucked behind her ears, and shook it until it almost covered her face. Then she peered at him through the dark curtain which it made in front of her large, brown eyes.

'I'm going to be a witch!' she said wickedly. 'The Witch Iseulte of Ty Corn Du. There's a legend, or more of a local story really, about Ty Corn Du once having been the home of a great dyn hysbys, and that, one day, an even greater one will live here again. That's what gave me the idea of being a witch. *I* think that's the real reason why Pettigrew wants to live here. He's trying to turn himself into a dyn hysbys, and he thinks that if he could only live here, he would manage it. He's a fool! I know more about potions and herbs and things already, than he ever will.'

Simon looked at his omelette suspiciously. He had a vague feeling that he had seen her sprinkle something into that.

'Oh, don't worry,' she said, noticing his look. 'That was herbs from a bottle Meryl bought in the village. Anyway, look at the horn. It's still black and ordinary. They change colour and fizz or something in the presence of poison.' She picked it up and stuck the end into the remains of his lunch.

29

'There, see! It's still as black and cold as ever.'

He felt it again when she went to fetch some dried apricots and chocolate biscuits for their pudding. It wasn't cold.

'Why did she say it was cold?' he wondered. 'It's as warm as I am, but it's certainly not fizzing, and it is black.' When she came back he asked her about the colour. 'I thought Unicorns had white horns,' he said.

'Oh, no, not always. They even have red ones in stories from some countries, or red, white and blue. Mr Smith told me. He told me about the poison bit, too. He insists on standing it on the table every time he eats anything I cook. Honestly! What a comment on a girl's cooking!'

Simon laughed. 'Your omelette was as nice as my mother's,' he said. 'And she's not a bad cook at all.'

She chewed an apricot, staring at him thoughtfully. 'They say that your father is ill. Is he?' He nodded and looked away. 'What's he got?'

'I don't know. They haven't told me.'

'That's bad. They never tell you about anything really serious.'

'I know. I came home from school one day, and Mum wasn't there. There was just a note saying that Dad had been taken ill at the office. Then my Aunty Vi and Uncle Sam came, and I guessed that Dad was very ill from the way they kept whispering and staring at me when they thought I couldn't see them.'

'I can just imagine it,' the girl said gloomily. 'They mean well, but they have the same shattering effect as a cow trying to tiptoe over wine glasses. But go on! What happened then?'

'Well, nothing, really. Mum didn't come home until lunch-time the next day. She looked awful. You know. White, with black rings and puffy eyes and lines down her face where she had been crying. But dad wasn't dead. I was afraid he would be, but he wasn't. He's very ill, though, I think. He still looks ill . . . but, now we're here, on the mountain, I think he feels a bit better. He was smiling today, when he went off for his check-up, and he hasn't smiled for months. He just looks . . . looks, he looks as though he's sort of listening to something inside himself all the time.'

'Your mother's all right, though?'

'Oh yes. She's fine! She's just a bit extra fussy now, that's all. What about your people?'

'Oh, I live with Meryl during the holidays. I'm at school in the North all term time. Father works in London. He doesn't come down here very much.'

'What about your mother?'

'She's gone off,' she said, pushing back her chair noisily. Simon thought she made it sound as though her mother was like food which wasn't wholesome any more. 'Come on! You can help look for more eggs for Meryl. She'll be home in a minute, and you've eaten her share.'

The cobbled yard at the back of the house filled with speckled hens as soon as they stepped on to the thick, grey slab of slate outside the kitchen door.

'Stupid birds!' the girl said. 'It's one track minds

31

they've got . . . their stomachs.' She opened a side door and dipped a scoopful of grain from a big, brown sack. 'There you are! Thoroughly spoilt!' she said as she flung it at them. The hens were immediately joined by hordes of sparrows, swooping down from the roof.

Simon waded through them all, and followed her to one of the tumble-down, stone barns on the far side of the yard. There they searched through a mound of straw until they had found four brown eggs. They heard Meryl's car pull up just as they were carrying them back into the kitchen.

'Fred!' Meryl called. 'Fred! I'm home.'

'Who's Fred?' Simon asked.

The girl scowled. 'Me!' she grumbled. 'I'm Fred. Frederika, really.'

'You told me you were called Iseulte!'

'Well, who ever heard of a witch called Fred!'

Simon liked Meryl as soon as he saw her. She was very tiny and quick, with long, black hair and big, brown eyes, like Fred's. She had nice, white teeth when she smiled, and would have been pretty, he thought, if she hadn't had such straight, black eyebrows. They were thick and bushy, almost like a man's, and made her look a little unusual.

She stacked an armful of paintings against the coat-rack in the hall, before shaking hands with him.

'Did you sell any?' Fred asked.

'Three of the chocolate-box variety,' she said. 'That's all the Oysters want, they tell me.' Fred explained that Meryl was an artist.

32

'An unsuccessful and very hungry one,' Meryl added.

They showed her the eggs, and she set about scrambling them while they wandered outside again. Simon touched the horn as he passed it, and suddenly decided that he must carry it around with him, just for a while. He picked it up, and laid it over his shoulder. The wide end fitted snugly into the palm of his hand.

The jungle of garden at the back of the house was hedged in on three sides by more huge rhododendrons. There were many more kinds of flowers than Mother had in her garden, and a lot of herbs, too. Fred knew all the names. She pointed out valerian, montbretias and hydrangeas, basil and rosemary, and they trod carefully on the wild thyme at the foot of an old sundial, until the air hung heavy with its scent.

'Come into the Summer House,' Fred said, leading him towards a raised platform of slate tiles, fenced around with a trellis of rotting branches which seemed to be held together only by a thick growth of climbing roses and Russian vine. 'There's a gap in the rhodos behind this, and you get a good view of the mountain,' she said, as she scrambled up, pushing aside a thick mass of creepers.

Simon lifted the horn on to the slate floor, then climbed up beside it. He picked it up and held it cradled in his arms as he followed Fred through the gloom to the far side of the shadowy, cobweb-filled space. She pulled the vine until she had made a gap as big as an average-sized window. Sunshine streamed in.

Simon hadn't looked at the mountain from a distance before. He had seen it from his bedroom window, a wide stretch of green and brown, scattered with large grey carns and boulders. He had looked at it from the beach, a mass of wild moorland rising to a grey peak, with the village nestling in its shadow. Now, he felt as though he was seeing it properly for the first time. The carn of stones shone silver-blue in the sunlight, below it a vast blush of purple spread outwards and downwards to the brown of the wild moor, and the dark green of the rough hill pastures. The village lay like a friendly, grey shadow, winking at him from its sunlit windows.

And halfway up the wild slope just where the purple blended into the brown and green, shone a bright, blue light. It was more blue than the carn, and as bright as a star at midnight. As he gazed at it, the horn began to move in his hands. He held it lightly, and let it twist. It twisted and pushed against his hands, forcing them apart. It jerked a little, and he gripped it, afraid that he would drop it. It pushed harder, making him lean forward, reaching, arching over it. Its base dug painfully into his side. He felt beads of sweat standing out on his forehead. His back was suddenly icy cold. He shivered.

'Whatever's the matter with you?' Fred was staring at him, wide-eyed.

'It's . . . it's . . . the horn,' he said. 'It's making me do it. It's making me point it at that light over there. That blue light on the mountain.'

4 Fred Plans and Simon Worries

'It was just like water divining,' Fred said. 'I watched a man do it, last Summer, with a forked twig. It twitched just like the horn did, and pushed his thumbs up as it pointed at the water. It was right, too. They dug a well, and found a whole underground spring.'

'But a unicorn horn wouldn't point at water, would it?' Simon said. 'I wonder what it was pointing at?'

He was still feeling very shaky. Fred had stopped the horn. As soon as she put her hand on it, it no longer behaved strangely. She was holding it now, across her lap, as they sat in the sun behind the Summer House. She looked almost as shaken as Simon felt.

'It could be pointing at a ruby,' she said. 'We know the two are linked somehow.'

'Or to poison,' Simon said, shivering slightly. 'There's a link with that too.'

Fred looked very solemn. 'It would be lovely if it was a ruby. Think what Meryl could do with it.'

'Yes, but what if it was . . . the other?'

'Well,' she said slowly, thinking hard. 'If it was a ruby we should claim it for our own, and if it was poison we should leave it where it was, or tell someone to come and clear it up. But whatever it is, I think we should try to find it.' Simon didn't say anything. The whole business frightened him. The horn had been marvellous at first. He had felt its warmth and power lying sleeping in his hands. But when it had begun to use that power, through him, he had been terrified.

Fred didn't notice that he was unhappy about it. She chattered on briskly, making plans.

'We can't do it today, it's too late, but tomorrow we'll climb the mountain and look for the light. This afternoon we'll see about teaching you how to get between my house and yours without falling foul of Bowcett and Pettigrew.' She looked him up and down. 'You're not very fit, are you! Don't you take any exercise at all?'

'I walk a lot, looking for insects, you know,' he said, 'but I don't play games much, because of my eyes.'

'Hmm. They're a bit of a bother aren't they. You can't see the ball, let alone the goal posts, I suppose. What a burden to carry around all your life!'

'Oh, I can have contact lenses when I'm older,' he told her. 'It should be much better for me then.'

'That's some consolation for you,' she said, 'but it doesn't help us now. I think the best plan will be for you to avoid Pettigrew and Bowcett, and at the same time , we'll try to get you fit, so that if you do meet them, you will at least stand some chance of being able to run away. One good thing is that you're not fat.' She stood up. 'Come on! We'll put the horn back on the wall, and tell Meryl where we're going.'

They didn't take Gwenhwyfar, but Bedwyr crept out of his den beneath the rhododendrons and followed them. Fred explained that there were several secret routes between the two houses, all of them using quiet footpaths which the Oysters didn't know.

'I'll show you the shortest way today,' she said, 'and we'll see about the others tomorrow, if we have time. We'll have to follow the roads here and there. When we do, we'll run. It'll do you good.'

They walked along the avenue, and turned right into the road to the beach. Fred broke into a jog-trot, and bullied him into keeping up with her. He was glad that it was all down hill. Even so, he had a terrible stitch in his left side by the time they reached the Golf Club.

'We can walk past this afternoon,' Fred said, 'but if you come this way at lunchtime, or in the evening . . . run! Pettigrew's often here then.'

She dived off abruptly into a hidden path, leading down a steep slope through bracken which reached up to his shoulders.

'I'll never find this again,' he thought, but next minute he recognized the wider path which they joined as the one where she had waited for him with the donkey. Then he concentrated on trying to remember the way, and forgot about his stitch. They were hidden perfectly by dense undergrowth until they reached the road, and had to cross the bridge which spanned the estuary.

Fred pointed out a well-trodden path on the other side of the road.

'That's an Oyster Track. It leads along beside

the river to Pettigrew's cottage. Needless to say, we won't be going that way. He lives up there all summer, then goes and leaves it empty all the rest of the year. That's what he would do with our house. Leave it empty, and dead, all year except for four months, when he would cram it full of his horriblest, noisiest Oyster friends.' She began to run across the bridge.

'She's going much faster,' Simon thought. 'She's afraid Pettigrew might be around.'

It wasn't a nice thought, for, if Pettigrew was there, Bowcett might be too. His knees felt as though they would buckle and give way at any moment, but he made himself trot after Fred. He glanced down at Bedwyr and wondered which of them was panting most.

Fred dived into the bushes again on the far side of the bridge, and waited for him.

'We could go along the road. There's a path which runs straight along the mountain to your house, but we'll go this way today. I want to show you something in the village.'

They followed another well-hidden path until they reached one of the tarmacked side-roads which led up to the main street.

'It's something in the antique shop,' Fred said. 'I only hope the place isn't full of Oysters. I'm only allowed to browse around when it's empty, and Bedwyr is strictly banished.' She took a careful look up and down the street before leading him across it. Then she made him run again, along the pavement, into the shelter of the antique shop doorway.

'Why are we running again?' he asked.

'I saw a lout who could have been Bowcett. It's all right, though, he walked off towards the dinghy beach. I don't think he saw us.' She peered through one of the bottle-glass panes of the door window. 'Good! Absolutely empty! Stay there, Bedwyr!' She pointed at a patch of shade in the doorway, and he sank into it, glad of a chance to rest.

The shop was cool and full of strange shadows thrown by tall dressers and old spinning wheels. Simon would have liked to look at the spinning wheels, but Fred hurried him past them to a shelf full of big, dusty books.

'I found it the other day. It's called "Myddfai Historian", but it's not about History.'

'What is it about?'

'I'm not sure. I didn't have time to read more than the index. A crowd of Oysters came in and I had to get out of the way.' She searched the shelves. 'Oh, here it is! It's been left out, away from the others.' She lifted down a huge, black book. 'Now, look at the index! I don't know what you think, but I think this is a book about magic. Look!' She pointed at the chapter titles. 'Ye Afanc, Ye Goldenne Willowe, Blue Stonnes of Preseli . . . all to do with legends or mysteries . . . and . . . page seven hundred and seventy seven . . . the page with the most magic number . . . Ye Blacke Horne. Our horn!'

She quickly found the page, and held the book open in her arms, Simon stepped closer and peered around her shoulder. The page was dry and yellow with age, and the print, very, very small and black and close.

'Can I hold it?' he said. 'I think I'll need to get very close if I'm going to read it quickly.'

Fred was about to argue, but, just then, Bedwyr gave a loud yelp and began to bark.

'Someone trod on him!' she said indignantly. She thrust the open book into Simon's arms and rushed out muttering about 'Oysters'.

The book was much heavier than he had expected it to be, but he managed to hold it steady against his chest. He bent his head, and peered closely at the script. It was very old, it used 'fs' instead of 'ss', and the spelling was funny.

'Ye olde manfione knowed af Ty Corn Du if fo named becoffe of ye horne of ye Unicorne sich hangeth inne ye greate halle,' he read. 'Ye horne belongedde to ye Grande Wizarde sich dwellede thereinne . . .'

He read no further. He was suddenly aware of someone else in the shop. Someone who must have come in very quietly. Someone who was creeping towards him through the shadows . . . It was Billy.

Billy grinned unpleasantly. 'Jonesy, Jonesy, Jonesy,' he hissed in a loud whisper. 'Cornered alone! And what have we here? What's this it's reading? My book!' He advanced until his chest pressed against the edge of the book opposite Simon. Then he pushed. His face was close to Simon's. He leered at him, straight into his eyes. Simon backed away. He felt the bookcase against his back. He was trapped. Billy leant hard. The book seemed to be cutting into his ribs. He could

hardly breathe.

'It's . . . it's not your book,' he gasped.

'Ah, but it is my book. It's been put aside for me, saved specially. Now I've come back with my money, and what do I find? Old Four Eyes has got its greasy, little paws on it.' He grinned again. 'Now, what if Old Four Eyes was to damage it? I wouldn't have to pay as much, would I?'

Simon almost stumbled forward as Billy stepped back suddenly. He felt, rather than saw, the big boy's hand reach out to pluck at the page and tear it. He slammed the book shut. The tips of Billy's fingers were trapped inside. He heard the gasp of pain and fury.

'He'll kick me this time,' he thought, and braced himself for the shock.

A voice as smooth as oil on water broke the tension. 'Billy!' it said softly and accusingly. 'What *are* you doing, Billy!' Just for a moment, Billy seemed to cringe. He turned away, looking rather shamefaced and guilty.

'Aw, nothing, Mr Pettigrew,' he said, with just the hint of a whine in his voice. 'This little creep's got my book, that's all.'

Pettigrew! Simon peered at him through the gloom. He was a tall man with broad shoulders. His dark hair lay, thickly oiled, flat against his head. Simon couldn't really see his face. It was hidden by thick, dark glasses. But he could see his thin, pale lips. They scarcely moved as he spoke.

'Well! So he has! . . . But we mustn't hurt him, must we, Billy . . . even though we were stupid enough to let him jam our fingers . . . our *clumsy* fingers . . . in the book . . . The book which we *must not* damage.'

'I didn't mean that, Mr Pettigrew. Honest! I wouldn't have torn it, really.'

Pettigrew seemed to loom over them in the darkness. 'Give the book to me, child,' he said. Simon handed him the book, squirmed past him, and scurried out.

Fred was nearly in a state of panic. 'It was Pettigrew and Bowcett! Did they catch you? That lout! He trod on Bedwyr's paw, deliberately! And Pettigrew tried to kid me that he was sorry for him. What did he say to you? Did he *do* anything?'

Simon began to tell her what had happened, but she suddenly grabbed him and rushed him along the pavement to the doorway of the butcher's shop.

'It's them!' she whispered loudly in his ear. 'They're coming out.' They hid, quietly, hardly daring to breathe. Then Fred peeped around the edge of the doorway and watched them. Simon saw her frown. 'Bowcett's carrying a big, black book under his arm,' she said. 'It looks very much like the Myddfai Historian.'

'It is!' he whispered. 'He went in especially to buy it.'

She looked quite worried. 'They're taking it to Pettigrew's cottage!' she said. 'They must be! The Bowcetts always stay on the other side of the village. It's Pettigrew who wants it, not Billy. He must have persuaded Billy to buy it. But why? Why does he want it?'

They waited until Pettigrew and Bowcett had disappeared down the road to the bridge, then they made their way through the village. Fred still looked worried, but, as soon as they reached the mountain, Simon felt all right again. He was very tired, and his ribs were sore, but he felt safe and happy.

They sat on the seat in his front garden, looking up across the bay, as they ate the sandwiches Mother had left. Fred was interested in the garden.

'You've made it very tidy,' she said, 'but it's still beautiful. I'm ever so glad you're letting the rhododendrons grow again. There always used to be a big clump of them here, just like ours, but the last people cut them down.'

'There are a lot more coming up in the back garden,' Simon said. 'Mother says she's never seen anything like it. The ground is absolutely full of rhododendron roots. She says they'll take over the garden if she's not careful.'

'Let's have a look,' Fred said, and he took her around to the other side of the house, but when she got there she forgot about the garden and looked at the mountain instead. 'You've got a jolly good view of the hillside from here,' she said. 'Can you see any sign of that light?'

He couldn't, but when she had gone he went up to his room and looked out of the window. There was no glimmer of blue anywhere on the mountain.

'It's gone,' he thought. 'Or perhaps it's hidden by trees or stones. Maybe it will show up later, shining out from behind something. It's easier to see lights at night.'

He stayed up until it was dark, in spite of feeling

very tired. He sat on the low window-sill and gazed out at the dim, shadowy slopes towering above him. An owl called, and sheep bleated from somewhere right on top. Their house was the highest in the village. It should be possible to see any light on the mountain from his window. There were car head-lights, occasionally, on the mountain road. But there was no brilliant, blue light at all.

Then he began to worry. 'I wonder if I could only see it because I was holding the horn,' he thought. 'Oh dear, I hope not.' He wanted to find the light, but he dreaded having to hold the horn again. He had hoped that he would never have to. It didn't feel nice.

But, the more he thought about it, the more he was afraid that this must be true, and he would have to go through it all again. Then he suddenly thought of something else which worried him even more. Had Fred seen the blue light? He sat staring out at the gathering darkness, trying to remember what she had said about it. Had she said anything about what it looked like? Had she actually said that she could see it?

'She must have been able to see it!' he thought. But he had an awful feeling that she would have made a lot more fuss about it if she had.

5   *The Sunlit Islands*

Mother woke him with a cup of tea and the news that there was an old, off-white dog, sitting, panting, on the back step.

'Bedwyr!' Simon shouted, and rushed downstairs to let him in.

Bedwyr was pleased to see him. He leapt around a lot, bouncing high enough to take a quick lick at his chin. But he wouldn't come into the house. He wagged his stubby tail politely in thanks for the invitation, then ran a few paces away and barked over his shoulder.

'He's been sent to fetch you,' Dad said, leaning out of the bedroom window. Simon laughed up at him. Suddenly his father looked wide awake and almost well again.

'Hang on, Bedwyr!' he shouted. 'I've got to get dressed.'

'And have your breakfast,' Mother called.

His father was sitting on the step beside the dog when Simon went out with his cornflakes in one hand and a chunk of toast in the other.

'He's lousy!' Simon warned him.

'Now you tell me!' Dad said, immediately beginning to scratch. He laughed. 'I should have guessed. I had a Wirehaired Terrier who threatened us with a coat like that, when I was about your age.'

'You never told me!'

'No, I haven't, have I. There's never seemed to be time before.' They talked about the terrier while Simon ate his breakfast.

Bedwyr took him straight to Fred and Gwenhwyfar, where they were both dozing in the sunshine beside the footpath which led up on to the mountain.

'What kept you?' Fred asked crossly.

'Breakfast. I woke up late,' he explained. 'I stayed up until it was dark to see if I could see the light.'

'Well done!' she said. 'That was good thinking. Where do we go from here?'

'I don't know,' he said, feeling that he was letting her down badly. 'I couldn't see it. I . . . I think I could only see it yesterday because I was holding the horn.'

'Oh, brass bedknobs!' she said crossly. 'Why didn't I think of that!'

'Could you see it?' he asked.

She looked at him sharply. 'I wasn't holding the horn,' she snapped.

'No. I meant afterwards. You held it then. You took it away from me.'

'I didn't look.' She sounded very annoyed, and turned her back on him to call Gwenhwyfar, before he could ask any more questions.

'She's cross because she didn't see it,' Simon thought. 'She should have looked for it when I told her about it. I wonder why she didn't?' Then he

began to worry again. 'I wonder if she did try, but she couldn't see it. I wish she would tell me. I can't ask again.'

'You can walk,' Fred said, as she climbed on to the donkey. 'It will be the start of your exercise today.' She made him run, and he was exhausted by the time they reached the heather line. He almost fell on to a flat, grey, triangular slab of stone which lay flush with the hillside, its neat, straight edges overgrown with bracken on one side, dense, prickly gorse on the second, and purple heather on the third. It felt deliciously cold. He lay, face down on it, pressing one hot cheek against it, then the other, until he felt cool again. Then he turned over on his back and felt the heat drain away from him.

Fred got off Gwenhwyfar and came to sit beside him.

'There's not much point in looking for the light without the horn,' she said, gloomily. 'I'll bring it tomorrow. Today, we'll just climb to the very top and look at the view. It's clear enough to see Lleyn and Bardsey Island today, not that you'll be able to, but I will. I'll help you identify larks and pipits by their song, to make it more interesting for you. We might even hear a raven or a buzzard.' She pointed down the hillside. 'Can you see your house?'

'That white building nearest to us, you mean? Yes. I guessed it must be ours, it's the nearest one to the mountain.'

'You'll never be able to see mine, though. I can't see the actual house, but I can see the avenue. It's directly in line with your house from here. If I squint and don't look sensibly, it almost looks as though it's growing out of the middle of your roof. Oh, there's someone in your window, waving something pink.'

'Mother,' he said. 'It's her apron. She likes to wave. I'd better wave back.'

Fred waved too. She sighed, and Simon thought that she looked a bit fed up.

'Sorry about thinking that it was me and not the horn,' he said.

'It's not your fault,' she told him. 'And, anyway, it was you too.' She stood up, shivering. 'Come on! I'm getting cold sitting here for such an age. My behind's freezing! I'll walk with you now, it's a bit steep for Gwen to carry me from here on.' She looked around for Bedwyr. 'Where's that dog gone?' She whistled the piercing whistle, with two fingers in her mouth, and Bedwyr came out backwards from beneath the gorse bushes, his tail wagging with pleasure, his face covered with fine, brown earth. 'He's a devil for rabbit holes,' Fred said.

She made the walk to the top very interesting for him. He heard the skylarks, as she had promised, and a stonechat, which he also saw, but only as a dark shape flitting across the tops of the gorse bushes. He, in turn, pointed out insects to her. They found several violet ground beetles, and a drinker moth caterpillar, and there were honey and bumble bees everywhere. At the very top, among the grey stones of the carn, Fred showed him bilberries, and he found some insects which he had never seen before. Fred thought they were hornets, but he was sure that they must be some kind of large hover-fly. They were striped, dark brown and bright yellow, and hovered, buzzing loudly, before dashing off suddenly in an unexpected direction. They rested on the stones, too, and he sat down carefully beside one to study it.

The stone was warm and rough against his legs. It was covered with lichen, and he thought how nice the insects looked in the sunshine, surrounded by round patches of grey and black and orange. He didn't bother to look for the Lleyn Peninsular and Bardsey Island. He didn't even think about them until Fred reminded him.

'It's more misty in the distance than I thought it

would be,' she said. 'I can see them, but only just, like shadows of clouds on the horizon.'

She was sitting right on top of the grey carn, with Bedwyr beside her. The breeze was blowing her hair back from her face. The old dog squinted as it unfolded his neat little ears, and stood them on end, making him look half asleep and wide awake at the same time. Simon climbed up and sat down beside them, turning his face to the wind.

He saw the Islands immediately. There were seven of them, rising through the white mists, their summits bathed in golden sunshine. Five of them were flat topped and thickly wooded. He could see the trees quite clearly. The other two rose steeply in jagged pinnacles of rock which glittered as though they were studded with jewels and veined with seams of gold. The most distant one seemed to be completely bare except for a thin line of tall pine trees which zigzagged up the gaunt, rocky face. The other one was absolutely beautiful. Sparkling cliffs rose from slopes covered with rhododendrons and azaleas in full bloom, a riot of reds, pinks, orange and white against the glossy, dark-green leaves. And on the topmost peak of the mountain behind the cliffs, stood a castle. Its smooth walls were of shining gold, the roofs of its seven turrets were tiled with silver, and from the point of each turret hung a long banner, streaming gently in the breeze.

He counted the banners carefully. 'One, two, three, four, five, six, seven. Red, orange, yellow, green, blue, indigo, violet. All the colours of the rainbow,' he whispered, and, as he watched, a

perfect rainbow appeared linking the two tall islands. 'They're beautiful,' he whispered.

'What are beautiful?' Fred asked.

'The Islands out there in the mist. They're not shadowy now. Look at them! Look at that rainbow!' He turned and smiled at her joyfully. 'I've never seen anywhere so beautiful,' he said.

Fred's face was a deathly white colour. She was staring at him, open-mouthed. She looked away quickly and stared out to sea.

'Y-yes. They're . . . very beautiful,' she said, shakily, her lips quivering, and one large tear squeezed out of the corner of her eye and fell on to her lap.

Then Simon realized that she couldn't see the Islands. She was only pretending to see them. He looked back at them. They were still there. They were still beautiful. But now they frightened him. Why could he see them? How could he see them? He shouldn't have been able to see them at all, not with his eyes. They were miles away, half hidden in the mists far out over the sea. But he could see them clearly, in every detail.

Fred spoke again, very slowly. 'I think the time has come for you to meet Mr Smith. Would you like fish and chips for supper?'

6   *Mr Smith and Tze Lu*

Mother fussed a bit when she heard that they planned to catch the bus to Fishguard that evening, but Fred phoned Meryl and persuaded her to come to fetch them home after supper. Mother had a quick chat with Meryl, and finally agreed. Dad liked Fred as much as he had liked Bedwyr, and Fred liked him, too. Simon thought that she looked very shy and nervous when he took her back to the cottage, but she was all right as soon as she saw how nice his mother and father were.

In the bus that evening Fred talked about being a witch. 'I can't decide what must be the best part of being a witch, the flying around on a broomstick, or the spells and potions and things,' she said. 'If I could decide, I might change my mind and be something else instead.'

'What do you mean?' Simon asked.

'Well, if flying's the best part, I might decide to be an air-hostess, but if it's the lotions and potions, I might go in for medicine, and cure people that way.'

Simon thought about it. 'I don't think being a doctor would be the same,' he said. 'You would *know* how to do the cure. You would have learnt all about it. But witches use magic, don't they?'

'Huh!' Fred scoffed. 'Tricks, you mean. *They* know what they're doing.'

'Sometimes, maybe, but they work magic, too, I'm sure. They know that they can do things but they don't know how they do them. It just sort of happens to them.' He thought about the horn and the Islands. 'I don't think it's very nice for them sometimes.'

Fred looked miserable. 'I suppose it wouldn't be bad being an air-hostess. The only thing wrong with it, as far as I can see, is that people don't take much notice of air-hostesses, except when they're flying with them, but people take notice of witches all the time, they're scared not to.'

'I don't think I would like having people scared of me,' Simon said.

'Oh, I wouldn't care, as long as it made them do everything I wanted.' She sounded very bossy, but when Simon looked at her, he saw that she was still miserable.

The bus stopped right outside the fish and chip shop. It was painted white, with bright blue blinds in its windows. Above the door was a sign, in big, black letters: 'J. L. Smith. Chips and Fish.' A long queue stretched right along the pavement. The smell was absolutely delicious. Simon saw Fred swallowing hard, and felt his own mouth watering.

Fred pushed past the queue, dragging him behind her. A man in a loose, dark-blue tunic and baggy trousers, with a small, round, dark-blue hat pulled down over his shiny, black hair, was standing with his back to them, turning crisp golden chips in a shimmering tank of bubbling oil.

'Mr Smith!' Fred called. The man turned his head quickly, and glanced down at them over his shoulder.

'He's the same colour as his chips!' Simon thought.

Mr Smith was Chinese. His slanting, brown eyes narrowed to tiny slits as he beamed a huge smile which was all big, white teeth. His nose was short and very straight, and his lips looked as though they had been chiselled carefully, like a statue's.

'Ah! Missy Fledalika!' he cried with joy, putting down his fish-slice, and bowing to her, a series of little nodding bows, with his hands tucked into the wide sleeves of his tunic. He said something in Chinese to a short, plump, almond-eyed girl, who was serving the queue, then disappeared through a door at the back of the shop. The girl grinned at Fred and winked, and Simon realized that Fred was trying her hardest not to giggle.

Mr Smith reappeared through another door on their side of the counter, and, still bowing rapidly, ushered them into a long corridor, dimly lit by a golden, hanging lantern. Simon felt rush mats beneath his feet, and could just see that the walls were hung with bamboo curtains. They followed Mr Smith along it to a door, outlined with a narrow crack of bright light. He flung open the door, and they all stepped into a room which seemed to Simon to be all space and fresh air.

It was lit by a chandelier of hundreds of tiny bulbs shaped like candles, which sent a cascade of golden bubbles of light rippling over the walls and the ceiling. Simon thought that the bubbles were bursting with tiny, tinkling notes, but the sound came from wind chimes which hung above the chandelier. The furniture looked very elegant, and there seemed to be huge vases everywhere, and a lot of books. But Simon thought that the best thing in the room was a beautiful Pekinese with long, soft hair, like brown and grey smoke. He was lying on a rich, red, velvet cushion, with golden tassles at each corner, right in the very centre of the thick, green carpet.

Mr Smith pulled off his blue cap and flung it into a corner. Then he turned to Fred with his arms held wide, and she jumped into them, shrieking with laughter.

'Ah ha!' he shouted, as he whirled her around and around. 'Missy Fledalika!' Simon looked on, astonished, but the Pekingese ignored it all as though he had seen it many times before.

At last, Mr Smith put Fred down. She was still laughing breathlessly.

'It's a wonderful act! You do it better every time, Smithy!'

'It's what the public expect,' he said, and Simon was even more astonished, for Mr Smith spoke exactly like one of the men who read the news on television. 'Now!' he said, turning to smile at Simon. 'You've brought me a guest. Hadn't you better introduce us, Fred?'

'Oh yes. This is Simon Jones, a friend of mine, who's come to live in Ty Corn Du Fach. Simon, this is Mr Smith.'

Mr Smith held out his hand, and Simon shook it politely. It felt hard and strong. Simon was surprised about this too, for Mr Smith wasn't very big, in fact, he looked as though he was quite thin inside his loose tunic. He also looked very kind, and somehow Simon had a feeling that he was very, very clever.

'You're not an Oyster, then, Simon?' he said.

'No. We're going to live here for always,' he told him.

'Will you like that?'

Simon thought before he answered. He felt that any question Mr Smith asked was meant to be answered seriously. Two days ago he would have said: 'No!', because there seemed to be nothing but Dad ill, Mother worrying, and Billy Bowcett bothering him. But now things were different. 'Yes, I think I will,' he said.

'But you're not sure?'

'Well. . . .' Simon looked at Fred for help. He thought that he had been brought here especially to tell Mr Smith about the Islands, but he didn't quite know how to tell him.

'He can see the Islands,' Fred said, bluntly. 'And the Unicorn's horn does odd things when he holds it.'

Simon felt uncomfortable as Mr Smith peered at him through narrowed eyes. It was impossible to tell what he was thinking. Then, suddenly, he smiled and laid his hand on his shoulder, shaking him gently.

'Tell me while you eat your supper,' he said kindly, and Simon knew that he understood exactly how he felt about it. 'Fred!' he commanded. 'Introduce Simon to Tze Lu while I fetch the food.'

'Come on!' Fred said. 'You have to do homage. He's very proud and full of his own importance.' They knelt together in front of the beautiful dog who stared at them out of his big, round eyes, and wheezed slightly as he raised his head to sniff in Simon's direction. 'Hold out your hand, palm downwards, then he'll get a good whiff of your scent. He won't forget you then, ever. He's very clever, very loyal and very brave. All Pekes are.'

'Is he as brave as Bedwyr?'

'Oh yes! He'd fight to the death for Mr Smith, he loves him so much. But he's old now, and Mr Smith says it wouldn't be right to let him try to do things like that any more.'

'Did he ever attack people, like Bedwyr does?'

Fred looked shocked. 'Bedwyr doesn't attack people! He practises the simple art of self defence. Mr Smith taught him. I thought you would have noticed that he didn't attack Bowcett. He simply defended you when I told him to, by confusing Bowcett with all sorts of unexpected tactics, like noise and rushing around all over the place.'

'Yes! So he did. I didn't think about it at the time, I was too scared.'

'You should never stop thinking, even when you're terrified, Mr Smith says. He never stops thinking, but then, he's a Superior Man.'

'He sounds superior. Is he a Mandarin?'

Fred laughed. 'No! They don't have them any more. And, anyway, he doesn't come from China.

He comes from Liverpool.'

'They don't talk like that in Liverpool!'

'Oh that's his Oxford accent. He picked that up at college. My father talks like that, so does Pettigrew, as you might have noticed. Now *there's* someone who could never be a Superior Man. Pettigrew! And Bowcett too! Both of them. They could never be anything but Inferior.'

Mr Smith came back in the room with two plates full of fish and chips.

'Everyone can be Superior if he tries,' he said. 'Confucius was quite definite about that.'

'Confucius.' Simon was immediately interested. 'I've heard about him. A boy at school had an American comic with him in it. He was a little man in a long, white shirt and a big hat, and every story ended with his saying: "Confucius, he say . . ." something or other.'

Fred looked disgusted. 'How dare they put him in a comic! He was one of the greatest philosophers that ever lived.'

Mr Smith laughed. 'I don't think he would have minded,' he said. 'But now, Fred, you mentioned Pettigrew and Bowcett. Has Simon met them?'

'Met them! I should say he has! Do you know, Smithy, that boy Bowcett bullies Simon terribly. He needs to be taught a lesson.'

'Is that what you came to tell me?'

'No.' Fred looked at Simon solemnly. 'I just thought that you ought to know about Simon.'

Mr Smith looked at him too, and Simon felt very hot and uncomfortable again. He felt that they both must think him odd, and he didn't like it. He was used to Billy Bowcett and other boys at school laughing at him because of his eyes and because he enjoyed maths, but he didn't want Fred and Mr Smith to laugh at him. He liked them too much. He looked at Fred. She wasn't laughing, in fact, she looked very sad. Then he looked at Mr Smith, and couldn't tell what he was thinking at all, but he wasn't laughing.

'Fred couldn't see the islands, could she?' he asked him.

'No.' Mr Smith shook his head gently.

'Couldn't you see the blue light, either?' he asked Fred.

'No.' She looked very miserable.

'It's a bit of a joke, really, when you think of it,' Simon said. 'I've never been able to see a lot of things other people can see, and now, all of a sudden. I'm seeing things no-one else can. They were there though, I didn't imagine them at all. I did see them.'

'Don't worry about it,' Mr Smith said. 'Tell me what happened, and tell me what you thought about it all.'

He listened to Simon in silence. Tze Lu climbed down off his velvet cushion, and pattered across to sit on his master's lap. He seemed to like to be as close to Mr Smith as he possibly could, and gazed up at him lovingly and adoringly, as he stroked him while he listened.

Mr Smith agreed with Fred. They must track down the blue light.

'The horn might not feel quite as bad next time, now that you know what it will do to you,' he said.

Simon hoped he was right.

'What do we do when we find the light?' Fred asked.

'That will depend on where it is and what it is. You can't decide what to do until you find it.'

'Can't you come too?' Simon asked.

'No. I don't think I could help you. Fred will keep you company. But I think you are the one who has to find it.'

'Couldn't you come to help us to decide what to do about it?' Simon had a feeling that if Mr Smith came with them, everything would be much easier.

Mr Smith smiled as though he knew what he was thinking. 'No,' he said. 'You do it on your own. But I will help with the decision, if you find that you do need help in deciding what to do about it, and I must confess I would rather like to know all about what you find as soon as possible. So, I think the best plan will be for you both to come here for a real meal tomorrow evening.'

'Ooh, goody!' Fred squealed with delight. 'He means a banquet,' she explained.

Simon thought it all sounded very satisfactory. 'I don't think Mother will fuss,' he said. 'Thank you very much. I'd like to come.'

Mr Smith was obviously pleased with his good manners. 'You have the making of a Superior Man, Simon,' he said. 'Would your mother be happier if I wrote a formal invitation?'

He wrote the invitation while they said goodbye to Tze Lu.

'He's called after Confucius's best friend,' Fred told Simon.

'He's a most Superior dog, isn't he,' Simon said. 'I wouldn't mind having a dog like this, but I'd need to have someone help me train it, if it was going to take care of me when Billy Bowcett was around.'

Mr Smith overheard him. 'This Billy Bowcett seems to be something of a problem to you, doesn't he,' he said. 'It seems to me that what you need is lessons in how to defend yourself, and I can help you there.'

Simon remembered what Fred had said about Mr Smith teaching Bedwyr 'the simple art of self defence.' He began to laugh.

'I would look pretty silly running around in circles, shouting, like you've taught Bedwyr to do.'

Mr Smith laughed too. 'You will have to shout,' he said. 'But maybe not with quite as much enthusiasm as Bedwyr does. I'll give you your first lesson when you come tomorrow.'

'What will you teach me?' Simon asked. 'Some kind of Kung Fu?'

'No. I'm a man of peace. We'll use good, old fashioned Judo.'

Simon decided that he liked Mr Smith very much indeed, and he liked him even more, when, just before Meryl came to drive them home, he took him to one side, and spoke to him quietly on his own.

'Don't worry about seeing these things which some people might say were not there,' he said. 'You have what is commonly called Second Sight. A lot of people without it would envy you if they knew that you had seen these legendary Islands.'

'They're in legends, are they?'

'Oh yes. There is a Welsh tale of enchanted islands hidden in the mist out over the sea. Fred knows all about them.'

'I wish she could see them. She's the one who ought to have Second Sight, not me. It would come in handy for her, when she's a witch, but it won't be much use to me when I'm a mathematician.'

'That's a matter of opinion,' Mr Smith said. 'It might make you a very extraordinary mathematician.'

'I would rather not have it, all the same. It's only women and girls who have it, usually, isn't it?'

'No, not at all,' Mr Smith's eyes narrowed mysteriously. 'Those Islands of the mist, those beautiful, golden Islands ... I have seen them too.'

7 *The Cold Blue Stone*

Simon was too excited to sleep. He lay staring through his window at the moonlit slope of the mountain.

'Fancy! Mr Smith can see them too!' he thought. It was comforting to know that he wasn't the only one who could. 'I don't mind being weird if I've got a weird friend. I wonder if Dad could see them? When he's better I'll take him up there, right up to the carn, and see if he can. I wonder who else can. I don't suppose Meryl can, and I'm sure Mother couldn't. I wonder who else can.'

Eventually, he did fall asleep, but then he had odd dreams in which Billy Bowcett and the Islands and the black horn were all jumbled up together, and nothing made sense. He was standing on the flat, cold stone all through the dream, and woke up to find that his feet were sticking out from under his quilt. He drew them back into the warmth, and lay awake again, thinking about the stone. There was something about that stone which didn't make sense, even when he was awake.

'Why was it cold?' he wondered. 'It was in the sunshine. It should have been hot. The ones at the top were much warmer even though they were right up there in the wind. But that one was sheltered, and right in the sunshine . . . and it was cold. Why?' He puzzled about it until he fell asleep again.

Fred had told him to meet her on the bridge after breakfast. He jogged all the way, taking the secret path which led across the lower slopes of the mountain. That way he avoided the village crowds, and Billy.

There was no sign of Fred on the bridge, so he sat out of sight, almost under the parapet, watching two small boys having fun in a flat-bottomed punt. They saw Fred before he did, and called to her and Bedwyr and Gwenhwyfar. She was riding down the path which led from Pettigrew's cottage. She waved to the boys and hurried the old donkey across the bridge at a quick trot. She hadn't brought the horn.

'Something terrible's happened!' she said. She looked worried. 'Come on, we must talk. Up on the mountain, where we won't be disturbed.'

Simon jogged after her, and didn't get left far behind. She waited for him on the mountain path.

'Why didn't you bring the horn?' he asked.

'Pettigrew's got it!' she said.

'How did he get it?'

'He stole it! Last night, while we were out. Oh, he left a note to say that he was only borrowing it, but it comes to the same thing in the end. He didn't ask, he just helped himself. He knew that if he did ask we would refuse.'

'What did Meryl say?'

'Oh, she's afraid of him. I told you about that. She just said she would ask for it back when he called again. But I went straight down to his cottage this morning to get it.'

'He wouldn't let you have it, though?'

'Oh, I wasn't going to ask him! I waited until I heard him chugging away in that awful, noisy boat of his, then I sneaked up and tried to get into the cottage.'

'But you couldn't.'

'No. The wretched man had locked and bolted everything. He had even drawn his curtains, right across! Most of them anyway. But I managed to peer through a chink in the living-room ones, and there was the horn, lying on a table . . . with the Myddfai Historian right beside it.'

'Billy left it with him!'

'Yes! I knew that was what would happen,' Fred wailed. 'I knew he only bought it because Pettigrew wanted to read it. And there must have been something important in that chapter about the horn.'

'Something about what the horn did when someone . . . different held it, perhaps.'

'Yes!' Fred was very upset. 'Something about what it was pointing at. And it must have been a ruby. It must have been something worth money. And it's not his. It's Meryl's!'

Simon was trying to think. 'It could be poison, not a ruby. Is he nasty enough to be interested in poison? Is Billy that nasty?' He decided that poison wasn't in Billy's line. He was just a straightforward bully. Then he remembered what Fred had told him about Pettigrew, and he thought about those few minutes with him in the antique shop. 'Pettigrew is nasty enough to be a poisoner,' he said. 'But if he wanted to poison anyone he could always buy some somewhere. Yes! I think the book must have mentioned a ruby.'

'It must have! And now he knows more about it than we do. And he's got the horn!'

Simon began to feel worried too. 'He comes from Myddfai, like I do, doesn't he,' he said.

'Yes!' Fred wailed again. 'And he's always hinting that he has some of the fairy blood in his veins. What if he's right? What if he can see that blue light? What if he finds it before we do? What are we going to do?'

'We'll just have to find the light before he does.'

'But how? You can't see it without the horn!'

'We'll have to try some other way, and I think I know where to begin looking. Come on! Up to that big stone we rested on yesterday. There's something odd about it.'

'What?' Fred asked.

'It's cold and it ought to be hot.'

They walked quickly along the narrow track, with Simon leading the way, answering Fred's questions over his shoulder. The day was warm and sunny again, and he soon began to feel hot. He found himself looking forward to the feel of the cool stone against his face. He tried to explain to Fred how he felt about the stone. She hadn't liked it. Its coldness had almost hurt her. But he had loved it. It had made him so comfortable, he would have been happy to stay, lying on it, all day.

'I wonder if you felt like that because you've got Second Sight?' she said.

'That's what I wondered.'

'It might not just make you see things I can't. It might make you feel things too.'

'Yes, sort of know things, somewhere.'

'Yes. Oh! There's something else about the stone too! It's in a straight line with our houses! Do you remember? I could see our avenue sort of perched on the roof of your cottage.'

'Yes! I'd forgotten that. And both houses are named after the Black Horn.'

They grew more and more excited, and Simon knew that it wasn't just the fast walking which was making his heart beat like a hammer when they finally arrived at the stone. He sat down on it right away, and placed both of his hands flat against it, his fingers outspread. Immediately, he felt his heart stop thumping. He felt comforted and relaxed. He sighed.

'It still feels great,' he told Fred.

She didn't seem to want to come too near it. She walked around, peering at it, studying it from a distance. Bedwyr disappeared beneath the gorse bushes, and they heard him yelping away quietly to himself as he dug furiously at his rabbit hole.

'Well, I might not be able to feel anything about it,' Fred said, 'but I can certainly see that there's something different about it. It looks as though it's been cut into that shape, for a start. The edges are almost perfectly straight, it's only the weathering which has worn them down to make them look natural.'

'There's nothing growing on it, either,' Simon said. 'No lichen of any kind, like there is on those on the carn.'

'That's because it's so cold, I suppose,' Fred said. Then she suddenly looked very excited. She

stepped closer and put out her hand to touch it very quickly, just for a moment. 'Do you know what!' she said. 'It's a slab of Bluestone. It's not quite the same as the other rocks around here, it must have been cut somewhere else and put here by someone. It could have been cut from the same place that Stonehenge came from.'

'And the light is blue,' Simon said, slowly. He felt as though he had just fitted the final piece into a jigsaw puzzle.

At that moment, Bedwyr gave a loud squeal. They heard him scrabbling frantically. There was a brief silence, followed by a soft, distant thud. Then he began to howl, a mournful, far-away, lost sort of howl.

'He's fallen down the rabbit hole!' Fred screamed. 'Help! Quick! We must get him out!'

8 *Beneath the Stone*

'Don't panic!' Simon said.

Fred tried to calm down. 'You're right. I must be Superior! But all these awful things keep happening, and wretched Pettigrew worries me so.' She knelt down and peered into the shadows beneath the bushes. Simon knelt beside her.

A neat, round tunnel led right under the gorse. It looked very prickly.

'I'm going in,' Fred said. 'Listen to him, poor lamb. If he can just hear my voice close above him it might be some comfort to him. You stay here and take care of Gwenhwyfar.'

Simon watched her wriggle into the hole like a long, striped caterpillar. He heard her pushing herself forward, complaining noisily. Then, after a while, she stopped.

'Are you all right?' he called, peering into the tunnel. He could just see her feet.

'Yes. I'm all right,' she called back. 'I've reached a pile of fresh earth. It must be Bedwyr's diggings. Oh, I can see the hole now. It's right beside the stone. There's sunshine coming through a gap above it. Bedwyr!' she called. 'Good boy! Fred's here. Good boy now.'

Bedwyr stopped howling and began to whine frantically.

'All right, old boy. Fred's coming. I'll soon get you ou . . . ou . . . out.' There came the noise of falling earth, and, with horror, Simon watched Fred disappear in a cloud of brown dust.

'Fred!' he called. 'Fred!' To his relief he could hear muffled coughing and choking somewhere, far away it seemed. He stood up and took a quick look at Gwenhwyfar. She was fast asleep. 'She won't go far,' he thought, and climbed up on to the stone. Then he saw it.

A faint gleam of blue light. . . . It came filtering up through the gorse, right at the topmost corner of the stone. He tiptoed towards it. He felt as though he had stopped breathing. He hardly heard Fred's voice.

'S . . . S . . . Simon,' she called. 'Simon, it's awfully cold down here. I c . . . can't stop sh . . . shivering. S . . . Simon! Can you hear me?'

'Yes,' he said softly. 'Yes, I can hear you. Can't you see it now, Fred? The light! It's here! You've fallen right into it.'

There was a deathly silence. He pushed at the gorse, and leant over to look down into the hole. The cold, greenish-blue light flooded out all around him.

'That's better,' Fred called. 'You've let in some sunshine.' She fell quiet again, but he could hear her scrambling around on the loose earth at the bottom of the gaping hole. Then suddenly her face appeared just a few feet from his own. It looked an odd, grey colour, bathed in the blue light. She

73

looked frightened. 'Simon! There's something queer down here. Something all pale and blurry. I don' know what it is. I w . . . want to c . . . come out . . . quickly. Get me out, please, Simon.'

He was just going to say: 'All right!' when he heard the noise. He thought it was just a ringing in his ears at first, then he listened properly. It wasn't in his ears. It was somewhere in his head. It came from the blueness of the hole, from somewhere in the icy blueness, but he wasn't hearing it with his ears. It was sounding somewhere inside him. It was a nice noise, like a deep-toned bell, a big bell, soft and mellow, and just a little sad.

'No!' he said. 'I can't go away now. Something's calling me. I must come in too.' And he jumped down, lightly, on to the pile of soft earth.

Fred clutched at him. 'You fool! Now we're all stuck!' she wailed, clinging on to his arm. He hardly heard her. He was so thrilled with the thing he could see there, bathed in the cold, blue light.

'Fred!' he said. 'You needn't be frightened. Can't you see it? Look! It's a Unicorn! A Unicorn held fast in a great block of ice.'

He walked towards it, with Fred still gripping him tightly. 'The light is more of a greeny, watery blue in here,' he told her. 'It must come from the ice.' He reached out with both hands and touched the ice. It felt hard and brittle and dry. He pressed his palms against it and leant hard, pushing with all his weight.

Fred gasped. 'I can see it! I can see it all too! When you do that I can see it. Oh Simon! Look at it! It's wonderful!'

They both looked. The Unicorn stood with its head held proudly, its black horn pointing upwards towards the bluestone roof of the chamber. Its long, silky, white mane seemed to have been tossing just as it was frozen, and the ice held it fast, floating above its smooth, white back. Its legs were placed squarely and firmly against the frozen floor, one fore leg was straight and firm, its neat, cloven hoof pointing forward slightly, but the other was raised high, and curved gracefully.

'It's got a curly tail!' Fred said. 'Oh, I do like its tail. Look at the tuft on the end!'

'It's perfect,' Simon whispered.

'Yes! Frozen and perfectly preserved, just like those mammoths they find in Siberia.'

'No!' Simon said. 'It's not like those mammoths. It's not like that at all. It's not dead. It's alive inside there. I can hear it calling to me.'

Fred leant close to him and looked down into his face. She didn't laugh or tell him not to be silly. She believed him.

'What do you think we should do?' she asked.

'It wants to get out,' he said. He could feel the ice changing beneath his hands. It wasn't hard any more, it was soft. He felt a trickle of cold vapour slip between his fingers, and watched it as it turned into a fine, blue mist which covered his hands for a moment then swirled away towards the hole, like a small wisp of cloud wafting out into the sunshine. 'Yes! I must let it out. I can let it out.' He suddenly knew that he could. 'The ice is melting. My hands are making it melt. They're turning it into mist.'

'Stop it!' Fred pulled his hands away. 'We must

think about it first. What could we do with it? Would it be safe?'

Simon turned and looked at her. 'It won't be safe here if Pettigrew finds it.'

'No, you're right. But we mustn't rush. A Superior Man thinks carefully before he does anything important. I think we should tell Mr Smith before we do anything else.'

9 Dad Remembers, Simon Decides and Mr Smith Agrees

Simon had to agree, but he didn't want to go. He wanted to stay where he was, inside the stone-roofed chamber on the mountain, with the unicorn. He wanted to stay there until the unicorn was free, and could leave with him. He didn't need Mr Smith to help him to decide what to do. But Fred insisted, and, finally, he thought it might be just as well to tell Mr Smith, although he knew that, no matter what Mr Smith said, he intended to set the beautiful creature free. It was something which he had to do.

Getting out of the chamber wasn't too difficult, mainly because Fred was so tall and agile. They scraped all the fallen earth into a pile beneath the hole, and when she stood on top of it, she could just manage to push Bedwyr out and heave herself after him. Then she helped Simon.

She came back to the cottage with him, and the rest of the morning was occupied by Mother fussing about their cuts and scratches. Simon thought Fred would be cross, but she seemed to like having someone washing her knees and dabbing her with antiseptic.

'We'd better meet at the bus stop, this evening,' she called happily to him when she eventually rode away to get lunch for Meryl. 'Wear your best clothes. A Superior Man is always very particular about dressing properly for banquets.'

Dad had slept in the garden all morning, but after lunch he stayed awake, and Simon sat on the terrace in the sunshine with him. The mountain rose before them in all its splendour. Simon felt fidgety. He couldn't see the flat stone from the terrace, but he could imagine it. He wished he was there. He wanted to be there, in the chamber, with the unicorn. He almost got up and went there. It was difficult not to, at first, but then Dad began to talk.

Dad looked very happy. He lay back on his sun-bed with his hands folded behind his head, and gazed up at the carn of rocks high above them.

'Do you know,' he said, 'I've never been up there. Ever since I first saw it, I've wanted to get there, but I never have, never.'

'When did you first see it?' Simon asked.

'When I was about your age. We had all come back to Myddfai to stay with my granny, Mam-gu, as we called her, and she arranged for us all to come here for the day. As soon as I saw the mountain, I wanted to climb it.'

'Why didn't you?'

'They wouldn't let me. Everyone else wanted to stay on the sands, and Mam wouldn't let me go on my own in case I got lost. I remember Mam-gu told me a lovely story to make up for not going. . . . I created a bit, I remember . . . but all the story did was make me want to go there even more. It was all about the mountain and a wizard.'

Simon sat quite still and held his breath. 'Can

79

you remember the story?' he asked.

'Well, let's see.' Dad settled back comfortably. 'It was about a wizard who lived at the court of a very wicked king, long, long ago, of course. I had an idea that he was Myrddin, but Mam-gu said he came from Myddfai, so I must have got that wrong. He was as great as Myrddin, anyway, and just as clever.

'Well, it seems that when he was a lad he witnessed the capture and slaughter of a Unicorn, and he never forgot it. They could never be caught with the usual sheer brute force hunting and slaughter method, you know. People used great treachery to catch them. They discovered that Unicorns like beautiful maidens, so they tricked them into being caught, using a maiden as bait. It came up to her, quite trustfully, and lay its head in her lap, and then the huntsmen were able to leap out and kill it. Absolutely horrible! And that's what this young lad thought too. And, when he grew up and another Unicorn was spotted in the forests near the wicked king's court, he knew he had to do something to make quite sure that it didn't suffer the same fate as the first one.

'Mam-gu said that he went looking for the Unicorn, frantic that he wouldn't find it before the huntsmen did, but he needn't have worried. For some reason best known to itself, the Unicorn came and found him. As soon as it saw him, it came up to him and knelt at his feet, and after that it followed him wherever he went. So, it was easy for him to lead it away from its enemies.

'But, of course, the wicked king's spies saw them and told the huntsmen, and they were chased right across the country, and finally arrived here, on the mountain. But they found that they were surrounded. There was no escape.

'However, the wizard tricked the huntsmen. By means of his great magic power, he hid the Unicorn where no-one could find it, and no-one ever did. To this day, it still lies hidden somewhere on the mountain, waiting for someone to find it.' Dad yawned. 'O-oh . . . this sunshine is doing me good.' He closed his eyes.

'But what about the wizard? What happened to him?' Simon asked.

'Oh, they banished him from the court. They were afraid to kill him, because of his magic. You know, they thought he might have powerful fairy friends who would avenge his death. He stayed here, near the mountain, for the rest of his life.'

'Why didn't he get the Unicorn out again? Why did he leave it shut up in the dark all those years?' Simon was beginning to feel quite upset.

Dad opened his eyes. 'Steady on!' he said. 'It's only a story.'

'No!' Simon said. 'Why did he?'

Dad looked at him strangely. 'I suppose the wicked king was still around somewhere, waiting, and hoping that he would let it out, so that he could have another go at catching it.' He shut his eyes again. 'Now! No more questions, please, Simon. I'm going to have forty winks again. . . . Oh, there's a rhyme Mam-gu taught us, too, a sort of jingle, about the story.

> *The Unicorn in days of old,*
> *Roamed o'er our hills, so wild and free.*
> *But now, in its chamber, blue and cold,*
> *It waits the hands with the twisted key.*

We had especially to remember it was blue *and* cold, not blue with cold, as we were tempted to say, and hands not hand, and twisted was important too. I once said twisting, and was severely put into my place.'

Simon was no longer listening. 'The hands!' he thought. 'The hands with the twisted key. My hands with the black horn. My family have been waiting for "the hands", and now they've come. I've got them! I ought to tell Dad.'

But he didn't get a chance. When he looked at

him again, Dad was already nearly asleep. Simon sat beside him as he slept.

'Fancy! Dad knew about it. And now I know why the Unicorn's there. But that king is dead now. I can let it out. I have the hands, and I'm going to see it free. I've *got* to. Oh, why do I have to wait and go to see Mr Smith!'

He was still wishing that he didn't have to go when he met Fred at the bus stop. He told her Dad's story as they waited.

'So now we know why the Unicorn's there!' Fred said. 'And where our horn came from.'

'What do you mean?'

'It must be the horn of the Unicorn which was killed. It stands to reason, that if the horrible king had it, it would sooner or later fall into the hands of his court wizard. And this court wizard made it into a key to set free the new Unicorn . . . a twisted key.'

'But it's the hands which are the important part.'

'Maybe.' Fred frowned. 'All the same, I wish Pettigrew hadn't got the horn. We must tell Smithy all about this, and see if he thinks we should try to get it back.'

They had to wait half an hour for the bus, which made Simon fret even more.

'It's such a terrible waste of time!' he thought. 'I should be there with it now. I could be working on that ice this evening.'

Fred grumbled about the traffic. It was bad. It seemed to be one long stream of cars and caravans flowing sluggishly through the village. It kept stopping, too, and to make everything even worse, one of these short delays brought Billy's father's car to a halt right beside the bus stop, and Billy was sitting in the back seat.

'Look! It's Bowcett!' Fred said. 'Oh! Brass bed-knobs! You should see his fingers. I think he's holding them up high so that we can take a good look. He's got plasters on two of them, at least! You must have slammed the Historian good and hard. Well done!'

But was it well done? Simon wondered. He knew why Billy wanted them to see his fingers. It was to let them know that he intended to pay back Simon for that encounter. He was relieved when the traffic began to move again, and, soon after, the bus arrived.

Mr Smith met them at the side door of the shop, wearing a loose, white jacket pulled in with a wide, black belt over even baggier trousers. He refused to listen to anything they had to tell him until the meal was served.

'Lesson first,' he said, and would not change his mind. Simon was very annoyed.

'It's all part of being Superior,' Fred whispered to him.

They had to change into outfits similar to Mr Smith's, but without the black belt, and Simon had to take off his glasses. Then Mr Smith took them into a small, well-equipped gym, which was tucked away behind the shop, and there Simon soon learnt to fall safely, but he found that learning to throw was much more difficult. Fred was quite good at it. She caught Mr Smith by the wrist as he pretended to punch her, and with a neat twist of her hips and a quick bend, threw him over her shoulder. Simon thought how useful it would be in dealing with Billy, but had grave doubts that he would ever be able to do it himself.

'I suppose that wasn't a complete waste of time,' he thought as he dressed. 'But I think I had better go on avoiding Billy until I've had time to practise it all quite a lot.'

The delicious Chinese banquet was spread before them, but Simon hardly noticed what he ate. 'At last we can talk about the Unicorn!' he thought, and forgot everything else. He let Fred tell Mr Smith how they found it, and how Dad had, quite innocently, told them how it came to be there. She did it very well, and he sat listening and remembering what it had felt like.

When she had finished, he realized that Mr Smith had been watching him intently.

'Now for a lot of talk!' he thought. 'Now for a lot of questions!' But Mr Smith only asked one.

'What's to be done about it, Simon?'

He was surprised, but he knew exactly what to say. 'I've got to set it free,' he said, quite simply.

Then Mr Smith smiled gently, and nodded. 'And you feel quite sure that you can.'

'Yes! I know I can. It's my hands, you see. They melt the ice.'

Mr Smith looked down at his own hands. 'I wonder if I could do that. I wonder if I could see it,' he whispered, almost to himself, and Simon realized, then, that Mr Smith was very, very excited.

'Simon could make me see it,' Fred said. 'He made me see the blue light. That's what I think was marvellous. I couldn't see it, before, not until he touched the ice. Then everything lit up!'

'But you could see the ice?' Mr Smith asked earnestly.

'Yes, and feel it! It's like a fridge in that little room. I could see the Unicorn inside it, too, but only blurry, like something in a mist. I wouldn't have been able to tell what it was if Simon hadn't made the light shine.'

'You realize what that means, don't you?' Mr Smith asked.

'Yes,' Simon said. 'It means that only the blue light is the magic. The ice and Unicorn are really there.'

'Brass bedknobs!' Fred said. 'So it does! Oh my goodness! And Simon says that it's alive!'

'Are you absolutely sure of that, Simon?' Mr Smith asked.

'Yes. I'm quite sure. I know it's alive. I don't know how it could be, but it is. It was asking me to set it free. I could hear it quite clearly, and I could understand what it was telling me, somehow . . . It wants to get out.'

'It wants to get out.' Simon had the feeling that Mr Smith was talking to himself again, so he said nothing. Suddenly he was glad that they had come. It was right to tell Mr Smith. He understood. He would help. They would need his help. He knew what Mr Smith would say . . . 'If it is asking you to set it free, then you certainly must set it free . . . and the sooner the better.'

10 *The Spell Begins To Break*

Mother fetched them that night. Simon was glad when she came.

'Now I'll soon be back on the mountain,' he thought. But she sat and chatted with Mr Smith, and paid homage to Tze Lu. He was surprised to see her fall to her knees without having to be shown what to do.

They eventually reached the village just as the last bus pulled into the stop. As Mother drove past it, he felt Fred stiffen beside him. She nudged him with her elbow.

'Guess who's getting off the bus?' she whispered.

'Who?'

'Bowcett!'

Simon knew why Billy had come home on the bus. It was because he thought he would catch him on it, and have him, captive, for half an hour. He didn't like to think of what that journey would have been like, or the walk home from the bus stop afterwards.

'I must be careful,' he thought. 'He might hurt me so much that I won't be able to help the Unicorn.'

They took Fred home, and stayed at Ty Corn Du for nearly an hour while Mother and Meryl chatted and looked at Meryl's paintings. Simon waited impatiently, and Fred took him out to the old Summer House where he could at least look at the mountain.

It was just a dark shadow against the deep blue sky. The lights of the village twinkled in a friendly way, and now and then, a car's headlights flashed across the sky, like a searchlight. And tonight Simon could also see a faint glimmer of blue half-way up the twilit slope. He told Fred.

'Bother!' she said. 'It must be seeping out through the hole I made.'

'It's not much,' he said. 'It's not nearly as bright as it was when I was holding the horn. It was almost like a flash then, but now it's just a glow. I don't think anyone would notice it, unless he was looking for it.'

'Well, Pettigrew will be looking for it, I'm quite sure! Huh! He won't even need the horn to find it now.'

Simon began to worry even more. He should have started work on the ice already. He must set the Unicorn free before Pettigrew could find it. *He* wouldn't want to help it escape from its prison. All he would want to do would be to kill it and take its horn and the ruby beneath it.

He thought of the solitary, beautiful Unicorn. It was such a gentle, perfect creature. He knew it was. He began to feel a dull anger about Pettigrew and Billy.

'I *will* set it free!' he thought. 'And no-one is going to stop me. I'm going to let it run away, out into the mountains, and be a delight to the world again.' He told Fred. 'I'm going to start early tomorrow. I'll stay there with it all day.'

'I'll stay with you,' Fred said. 'I won't be able to help you, worse luck, but we'll keep you company, me and Bedwyr. Smithy will come too, I expect, as soon as he can leave the shop. He was longing to see it. You could tell that.'

'Thank you,' Simon said. He didn't really mind if anyone came or not, he would have been quite happy to stay on his own with the Unicorn all day and all night, as long as he lived, if it needed him.

They heard Meryl calling from the house, and ran back in to her. Mother was looking very happy, Simon thought. She was carrying a small, un-framed painting. She showed it to him.

'Look what Meryl has given me,' she said. 'It's a water-colour of our cottage. She's going to do me a special big one to hang in the living room, then I can enjoy looking at my garden even when I'm sitting by the fire in the winter. I'm coming over here again tomorrow, to have a look at this garden. Do you want to arrange to come with me to see Fred?'

'We're going out all tomorrow,' Simon said. 'We've made plans already.'

To his surprise she didn't fuss at all, or ask any questions, but just chatted happily to Meryl about her own arrangements.

'She's like she used to be!' he thought. 'She's not miserable any more.'

She didn't fuss in the morning, either, but sang to herself as she packed a picnic for him.

'Now, Dad will be here all day, but don't disturb

him unless you have to,' she said. 'He'll enjoy being on his own for a change. You know where to find me if you need me. I've packed stacks of food and two cans of drink. It's going to be hot today.'

'I won't be hot,' he thought, as he took the duffle bag she handed him. 'Tell Fred I've gone on,' he said. 'She'll know where to find me.'

He trudged up the path to the cold stone, and dropped through the hole, into the blue light. The Unicorn looked even more wonderful than he remembered. He tiptoed across to the wall of ice and pressed himself against it, stretching his arms wide, as though he were trying to hug the Unicorn. He felt the ice soften beneath his hands, and saw the blue mist form between his fingers, and wisp away up through the hole.

'Have I really got magic in my hands?' he thought with wonder. He spread out his fingers, and settled down, relaxed and happy, and ready for a long day. And all the time he gazed and gazed at the Unicorn, and listened to its deep, bell-like voice.

Fred found him there when she arrived half an hour later.

'I knew you must have started on it,' she said. 'I could see the light glowing as I came up the track. It doesn't show up too badly in the sunshine, but, if we're still here this evening, not even the Oysters will be able to miss it. We'll have to block up the hole.'

He turned to face her, but kept his hands flattened against the ice.

'You must be freezing!' she said, peering into his

face.

'No I'm not,' he told her. 'I don't even feel cold, just coolish, but not uncomfortable at all.'

'I'm shivering already!' she said. 'But don't worry. I've brought my winter anorak, and the biggest flask I could find, full of scorching hot soup. What has your mother packed for you?'

She spent a happy few minutes rummaging through both bags, sorting out the food and arranging it into elevenses, lunch and tea. Then she climbed out to warm herself in the sunshine for a while. Bedwyr, who had been left on top, was very pleased to see her.

'Why don't you go down to my house and find something to block up the hole?' Simon suggested. 'There are all sorts of sacks in the garden shed.'

'Will you be all right?'

'Yes, go on. I'll be all right.' He turned, thankfully, to face the Unicorn again. He thought that it might possibly be just a little nearer to him than the last time he had looked at it. He gazed at it again. Fred was right. It had got an interesting tail. It curled like a pig's, but had a thick tuft of long hair at the tip, like a lion's.

Fred brought back Mother's hedge-cutting steps, as well as a huge armful of plastic sacks. She lowered the steps into the hole, then jumped in and fixed the legs firmly into the mound of earth.

'It'll be easier to get out, now,' she said. 'And Bedwyr can get in too, without me having to lug him around. She won't mind if we borrow them, will she? Now!' She stood back, with her hands on her hips, and surveyed the hole. 'Shall I or shan't I go back for more sacks? I'm not sure if it's worth trying to block it up with anything. Have you realized that you're turning the ice into smoke? At least, I think it's smoke. It's blue, and it looks like a bonfire, drifting up through the hole, and wafting away on the breeze.'

Simon leant back a little and studied the block of ice. A smoky mist had now begun to rise from all over its surface, not simply from where his hands were touching it. Fred leapt about, trying to catch the mist in her hands, but it swirled around her, always out of reach.

'It looks just like smoke,' she said, 'but it doesn't seem to have a smell at all.'

Simon sniffed. 'I can smell something,' he said. 'It's a bit like Christmas.'

'Brandy and cigars, or turkey and pudding?' Fred asked.

'No, not Christmas Day. Before Christmas, when you're getting ready for it. I know! It's spice! At least, I think it's spice.'

Fred looked excited. 'Spices and herbs, and all the mysterious things which went into the wizard's spell to make the blue light and keep the ice frozen and hold the Unicorn alive inside it. They must be separating out and escaping now, as you gradually break the spell.' Simon thought that she was probably right.

The day passed quickly, with Fred and Bedwyr eating all the food, and climbing up the steps every now and then to warm themselves in the sunshine, and Simon contentedly standing watching them when they were there and gazing at the Unicorn when they went away.

Fred inspected the block of ice every time she came back in. 'I'm sure it's a lot smaller,' she said at last. 'The smoky stuff is simply pouring off it now. It's a wonder no-one's seen it and called the Fire Brigade.'

'Is it very hot today?' Simon asked.

'Scorching!'

'Well, then, no-one's there to see it. All the Oysters are on the beach. They don't come near the mountain while it's good beaching weather.'

'You're right! They'll all be toasting themselves silly, or out sailing.'

'Sailing.' The word reminded Simon of Pettigrew and Billy. He felt uneasy. 'They don't sail all day.' He pressed harder against the ice, hoping that somehow he could make it melt faster. Fred must have noticed that he looked worried.

'Perhaps I had better fetch some more sacks,' she said.

'No. It's no good trying to block up the hole. The mist has got to escape, there wouldn't be room for it all in here. We'll be safe until they come in this evening. They'll notice it then, though, they're sure to. But I'll have the Unicorn free by then.'

Fred nodded doubtfully. 'Yes, I suppose you will.'

'Of course I will,' Simon said. 'I've got to.' Fred began to fuss. 'Are you sure you're warm enough? Would a hot drink help?'

'No.' He shook his head firmly. 'Thanks all the same. But you go out and have one if you like.'

He turned to face the Unicorn again as she

disappeared up through the hole. He studied its
horn. It was long and black, exactly the same as
the one Meryl owned. He looked at the place where
it joined the broad, white forehead. Was there

really a priceless ruby hidden there? He looked at its ears, pricked forward and alert. He looked at its eye. . . . The Unicorn was looking at him.

He looked back breathlessly. He felt so happy that he wanted to laugh aloud. The look in the gentle eye was as loving and adoring as the look in the eyes of Tze Lu when he gazed at Mr Smith. He listened to the call. It had changed. It wasn't lonely any more. The Unicorn was pleased to be near him.

11 *Pettigrew*

Fred and Bedwyr ate the last of the sandwiches at what they judged to be tea time. Soon afterwards they climbed out on to the stone again. Fred rushed back almost at once.

'The sailing boats are coming in! Quick! Stop making the smoky stuff. He'll see it.'

Simon stepped away from the ice, and began to follow her up the steps. Immediately, the Unicorn's voice changed. It called him, frantically.

'I'll have to go back to it,' he told Fred. 'It's unhappy because I've stopped, and I can't bear it when it sounds unhappy.'

'Tell it that you're only stopping for a little while.'

'I can't. I'll just have to keep touching the ice. It's happy then.'

Fred looked worried, but she didn't argue any more. 'Oh well, he probably saw the smoke hours ago, anyway. It must stand out like a beacon. We'll just have to hope that he doesn't come to find out what's happening until you've finished.'

She didn't mention Pettigrew again, but Simon knew that she was worrying about him. She never seemed to worry about Billy, only Pettigrew. He knew she was right. Pettigrew was the one to worry about. He was the really nasty one. And he was the one from Myddfai.

Fred seemed to be listening for footsteps all the time. She kept jumping up to look out of the hole, thinking that she had heard someone coming. He wished that she would sit still, but when at last she did sit on the bottom step for a moment, he wished that she hadn't, for she then began to look anxiously at the ice.

'You're not going to be able to finish it off today,' she said.

'Yes I am.'

'There's still tons of ice left.'

'I know there is, but I'm not going to leave the Unicorn until it's free.'

'You'll have to! You can't stay here all night. It's getting dark outside now. Your Mother will be worried soon.'

'You'd better go down and tell her I'm all right.'

'No. I don't want to leave you here all alone.'

'I'm not alone. I've got the Unicorn.'

'Yes, but it wouldn't be much help if . . . if . . .'

'If Pettigrew comes.' He finished the sentence for her.

'Yes, if Pettigrew comes.'

'He won't come.' Simon didn't really believe it. Nor did Fred when she echoed him.

'No. He won't come. He would have been here hours ago if he was going to come. He won't come.'

But he did come. Bedwyr heard him first. He had been sitting, dozing, at Fred's feet, but, suddenly, he stood up, wide awake. He gave a low growl. Then his lips curled back in a ferocious snarl, and he began to creep forward, up the steps, placing each paw carefully and quietly, glaring at something outside in the darkness. Then he sprang up through the hole, and a terrible commotion began.

Simon could imagine what it looked like. He had seen it before. Bedwyr was snarling and snapping at someone, running around and around in circles, dodging someone's kicking feet. It wasn't Billy this time. It was a man, on his own. They could hear him cursing and swearing at the dog.

'Pettigrew!' Fred said, her eyes wide with fear. 'I knew he would come!'

Next moment, the stone slab above them tipped and tilted. There was a loud shout of alarm. And Pettigrew crashed into the chamber with a great clatter of earth and stones. Fred dodged aside just in time, but the steps were flattened by his weight. He lay on his back, stunned, staring stupidly at the evening sky through the gaping hole above him. He was still wearing his dark glasses.

Simon stood still against the ice.

'I won't move away. He can't have it. He can't!' he thought. But Fred didn't stand still. With a loud scream, she leapt at the man and kicked him hard. Then, still screaming, she jumped on to the new pile of earth and tried to scramble out of the hole.

With surprising speed, Pettigrew rolled over on to his side and grabbed her legs. She fell backwards and began to punch and scream at him. Bedwyr leapt through the hole and joined in.

They were no match for Pettigrew. He knelt across Fred's legs, pinning her down while he caught her by both wrists. Then he hauled her to her feet, holding her at arm's length. Bedwyr attacked again. Pettigrew threw a well-aimed kick and hit him on the side of the head. He yelped once . . . then lay still.

The chamber was suddenly very quiet. Then Fred began to cry. Pettigrew ignored her. Still gripping her by one arm, he stepped towards Simon. Simon had never seen such an evil face. It shone with a strange green sheen in the light from the ice, and his dark glasses made the places where his eyes should have been look like deep, black caves in his head. His thin lips looked colourless, and when he turned sideways slightly, Simon was shocked to see that his ears were lobeless and pointed.

'*He* can't have the Unicorn,' he thought. 'Not him! Never!' He felt himself growing more and more angry. He couldn't hear the Unicorn any more. It had stopped calling. He could only hear Fred, sobbing bitterly. He looked down at Bedwyr, a pitiful, little heap of white fur. 'You devil!' he screamed. 'You ugly, greedy devil! You're not going to have it! I won't let you!'

'Why you little . . .' Pettigrew reached out his free hand to hit him. Simon grabbed it, stepped forward, twisted and heaved.

But something went wrong. He felt the man lift slightly, then the long heavy body fell on top of him, crushing him into the ground. He gasped for air. He couldn't breathe. He tried to scream. He couldn't hear. He couldn't see.

Then the weight lifted, and he could hear Petti-

grew laughing. It all sounded a long way away at first, then, gradually, his head cleared. A hard, bony hand grabbed him by the shoulder and pulled him to his feet.

'Up to Smithy's tricks, eh, you little shrimp! I should have known he would have a hand in this somewhere. Well, you run away now, like a good little fellow, and tell him to mind his own business. Off you go!' He gave Simon a push which sent him reeling towards the pile of earth beneath the hole. He fell on his knees beside Fred, who was trying to pick up Bedwyr. 'You'd better help young Frederika with that flea-ridden cur. Get him out of my way. I've work to do.'

Fred was still sobbing bitterly as she groped around beneath Bedwyr, trying to get her arms around him. Simon realised that his glasses were hanging from one ear. He hitched them back on properly and crawled across to her. The loose stones hurt his knees, but he was afraid to stand up. He felt dizzy and rather sick, and he still couldn't see clearly. His hand knocked against something very hard which rolled away in front of him and came to rest against Fred's feet. She turned and looked at it. He heard her give a little gasp. Then he felt something being pushed into his hand.

'The horn!' Fred whispered. 'It's the horn. He must have dropped it when he fell in!'

'The twisted key!' Simon grasped the hard, smooth base of the black horn. Immediately, he felt its power beginning to work. It jerked itself upright, and over in a complete arc, twisting his arms until it was pointing straight at the horn of the Unicorn. A jagged flash of bright blue lightning crashed across the chamber. And the ice shattered into a million, tinkling splinters.

Then the voice of the Unicorn filled the chamber like a mighty bell, and echoed back and forth from one wall to another. Simon felt as though his ears would burst. He saw Pettigrew rocking from side to side, his hands pressed against his head, his face twisted with pain.

Then he saw the Unicorn. It reared up on to its hind legs, pawing at the air, and crashed down again with a noise like thunder. The chamber floor shook and shuddered. Clouds of hot breath spurted through its flaring nostrils, and the look it gave Pettigrew was one of sheer hatred. It lowered its head, pawed at the ground, and charged.

Pettigrew threw himself aside just in time. The Unicorn leapt over him, up, out, through the hole, and away into the night . . . and freedom.

12 *Mr Smith Arrives*

'He's passed out,' Fred said. 'Quick! Let's get out of here before he comes-to.' The chamber was dark now that the ice had disappeared. They scrambled to the top of the earth pile, and just managed between them to lift Bedwyr out of the hole. Then Simon went back for the horn. 'Don't touch the stone,' Fred warned him. 'The blast must have loosened it. It rocks when you lean on it. Hurry! Hurry! He's scrabbling around already!'

She staggered off down the path, with Bedwyr, in her arms. Simon hurried after her. She didn't go far.

'It's no good! I can't hurry carrying Bedwyr, he's too heavy. We'll never get to your house before he catches us. Goodness knows what he'll do to us. He'll be raging mad!'

'We'll have to hide,' Simon said.

'Where? There's no cover at all, unless we crouch down in the bracken, and he'll soon find us.'

Simon looked around. 'We must go back, further up the mountain. He won't expect us to go that way. He won't look for us up there, not until he's worked out that we didn't go this way, and by that time Bedwyr might be on his feet again. Come on! He hasn't climbed out yet.'

Quickly and quietly, they hurried back past the blue-stone slab, keeping well away from the hole. Then they crouched down behind a thicket of gorse bushes, and watched for Pettigrew to appear. He pulled himself out, moaning, quietly, and stumbled around for a moment, still holding his head. Then he sank down to rest on the stone.

With a terrible scraping creak it began to tip up. Pettigrew flung himself clear, as it up-ended and slid into the hole in a cloud of dust. One corner disappeared completely, leaving the rest of the great slab sticking up into the air, like the sail of huge, stone boat.

They watched him lying face downwards in the heather. Simon couldn't see him properly, he was too far away, and it was almost dark. He wondered if he had fainted again, but, after a while, he saw him sit up and look around him. Then he stood up, and took a good look at the wide stretch of mountainside. He began to walk along the path, bending low, peering at the stony track.

'He's coming this way!' Fred whispered. 'You said he wouldn't! He's looking for us. He'll find us!'

'Be quiet!' Simon said. 'He might not see us in the shadow.'

Pettigrew stopped only a few feet away from them. He was muttering to himself.

'The ground's too hard, much too hard.' He stood up and looked at the mountain again. 'It's too dark too. I can't see a thing. I need that horn. Drat that brat for taking it!' He turned and strode off, back down the path, reeling as though he was still a little dazed.

'Phew!' Fred said. 'That was close! Bedwyr's just coming round. I was sure he would grunt, or something, and give us away.' She sat down and cradled the old dog in her lap. 'Poor boy,' she said. 'Poor old Bedwyr. Oh dear, I hope he'll be all right. Perhaps if we let him rest here for a while, he'll be able to walk as far as your house. It'll give Pettigrew time to go away, too.'

Simon sat beside her with the horn across his knees, and watched as Bedwyr struggled to his feet.

'It hurts when he stands up,' Fred said, as he sank back into her lap with a low groan. 'Look at the bump on his head, where that brute kicked him! He can't open his eye on that side. The other one's open though! He's looking at me properly again.'

Simon remembered how the Unicorn had looked at him. It had loved him as much as Bedwyr loved Fred, and as much as Tze Lu loved Mr Smith. He turned his head to gaze up at the carn, high above him. The Unicorn was up there somewhere, free to gallop over the mountain in the starlight.

'I wonder, when was the last time the Unicorn saw the stars?' he said. 'I expect it's happy now that it's out of its prison.'

'Yes!' Fred said. 'Wasn't it marvellous, the way the horn broke the spell! Did you see the way the Unicorn charged Pettigrew? It only just missed him, too, worse luck. It hates him as much as I do. I wonder why it hates him.'

Simon knew why. The Unicorn had seen Pettigrew hurt him. It was fighting Pettigrew for him because it loved him, but he couldn't tell Fred that, she would think he was boasting.

'It's nice to feel that it's free on the mountain. It's going to be wonderful for people to be able to see a Unicorn again.'

'Yes, I suppose so.' Fred sounded doubtful. 'As long as the Oysters don't find out about it. Imagine them all flocking up here, trying to spot it!'

Simon was horrified. He hadn't thought of that. He had only been thinking of the Unicorn, and how he felt that he had to set it free. He had thought that it wouldn't be safe in the chamber if Pettigrew found it, but he hadn't thought that it would still be in danger on the mountain. He hadn't thought of that at all. He began to worry again. He picked up the horn, and held it tightly in his hands.

It still felt warm. He could still feel power in it.

'It's not just meant to be a key for opening the prison,' he thought. 'It can still be used for something else. I wonder what else I can do with it?'

'Listen!' Fred said suddenly, reaching out to grip his arm. She touched the horn, and the feeling of power stopped immediately. 'Someone's calling. Listen!'

It was Mother. Simon could hear her calling his name.

'It's Mother,' he said. 'We'd better go down to her.'

'Pettigrew might not have gone yet.'

'We'll have to risk that. He wouldn't do anything with her around.'

106

'He would! He wouldn't let her bother him. We must wait a bit longer.'

They sat and listened. Mother's voice sounded louder.

'She's coming to find us,' Simon said. 'She sounds worried.'

'Brass bedknobs! She doesn't know about the hole! It's right beside the path. She might fall in!'

'We'll have to go and warn her.'

Fred crouched, shivering, cuddling the old dog to her. 'Bedwyr can't walk yet,' she said.

'She doesn't want to go. She's frightened,' Simon thought. 'You stay here and look after him,' he told her. 'I'll go and fetch Mother. Here!' He handed her the horn. 'You had better look after this, too, just in case Pettigrew jumps me and tries to snatch it back.'

'He won't want it any more now,' Fred said. 'It's you he'll want.'

'Maybe. But he wants the horn too. He said so. Didn't you hear him? I'd better leave it. Take care of it until I come back with Mother.'

He stood up and walked quickly down the path as far as the hole. It looked black and bottomless.

'It must have been awful for it, shut up in there for ages and ages,' he thought. 'I must make sure that it stays free, now, for always. The Oysters mustn't find it, or they'll catch it and put it in a Circus. And Pettigrew mustn't find it, either.' He didn't want to think of what Pettigrew would do to it.

He suddenly realized that his mother had stopped calling him, and that he could hear people talking, people on the path, walking towards him. One was his mother, and the other was a man.

'Dad!' he thought. 'No. It's not his voice. Mr Smith? No. I don't think it's him either.' It was Pettigrew. He was walking towards him through the dim, evening light, talking to Mother.

Simon almost turned and ran, but he didn't. It would only lead them back to Fred. He didn't walk forward either, but stood quite still, waiting for them beside the hole.

'Simon!' Mother called. 'Simon, is that you?'

'Yes,' he called back. His voice sounded like a croak.

'Simon, where have you been? I've been so worried.'

'I've been here, on the mountain, all day. You needn't have worried. I'm all right.'

'What have you been doing?' He didn't speak, but looked up at Pettigrew. His face was like a hollow-eyed mask, looming over him. Mother didn't wait for an answer. 'Simon, I don't know what to think. It doesn't sound like you at all, and I'm sure there's been some mistake, but this gentleman says that you've taken something which belongs to him.' She turned to Pettigrew. 'What did you say it was? A horn?'

'That's right.' His voice was as smooth as silk. 'A valuable, antique horn.'

'Have you got it, Simon?'

'No,' he said. 'I haven't got it any more, and anyway, it belongs to Fred's Aunt Meryl, not to him.'

Pettigrew stepped towards him. Mother gasped

and quickly placed herself between them. She put her arm around Simon's shoulders. Pettigrew towered over them, and, for one moment, Simon thought that he was going to hit her too. He could feel her holding him tightly. He knew that she was as frightened as he was.

'What can I do?' he thought wildly. 'What can I do?'

Then, out of the darkness behind them, came a voice. 'Can I be of any assistance, Mrs Jones?' It was Mr Smith, with Bedwyr in his arms, and Fred, carrying the horn, peeping out from behind him.

The danger was all over for the moment. Mother quickly explained to Mr Smith exactly what Pettigrew had told her.

'Yes, of course there has been a mistake, eh, Pettigrew!' Mr Smith said, and Simon could tell that he wasn't in the least afraid of him. 'Fred has the horn now. It is her aunt's property. She will return it to her.'

Simon looked at Pettigrew. He was furious. His thin lips were pressed tightly together, making his mouth into no more than a thin slit across the lower part of his face.

'There's going to be a fight!' he thought. But Pettigrew decided to talk himself out of the situation.

'Oh, that's all right, then, Smithy,' he said, pretending to laugh. 'As long as it's returned to Meryl. That was the only thing which worried me, having borrowed it, you know, and then mislaid it. I won't worry about it any more. Terribly sorry to have bothered you, Mrs Jones.' With one last angry glance at Simon, he turned and hurried towards the village.

'What was that all about?' Mother asked.

'Allow me to explain.' Mr Smith stepped forward and walked beside her.

Simon waited for Fred. 'How did *he* get up here on the mountain?' he asked. 'Did he come up past us?'

'No, he came down from the top. He always comes across the mountains, never along the road. Actually, he travels by Chinese Wheelbarrow. Don't ask me how! I don't understand, but he comes very quickly.'

'Is it magic?'

'I don't know. He won't tell me.'

'Did you tell him about the horn's magic?'

'Yes. He was pleased about the Unicorn being saved from Pettigrew, but he's worried about it being out there on the mountain.'

'So am I! It's not safe yet. I think Pettigrew is still after it. That's why he came back up the mountain, instead of going away down to the village. He was looking for the Unicorn, not us, but he couldn't track it because the ground is too dry and hard.'

'Brass bedknobs! I'm sure you're right! We'll have to hunt for the Unicorn. We must find it before he does.' She turned around and looked up at the shadowy mountain. 'But, wherever can it be? It could be anywhere, up there, or out on the sand, or over the hills and miles away. How ever are we going to find it?'

13 *Hunt the Unicorn*

Simon wanted to talk about the Unicorn with Mr Smith, but it was impossible. Mother took them all back to the cottage, where she insisted that Fred and Bedwyr must stay for the night, and, before he could protest, he found himself being pushed upstairs to bed. All he could do was rescue the horn from the corner of the kitchen where Fred had left it, and take it upstairs with him. He put it under his pillow.

'I've got to keep it safe,' he told himself. 'I've got to tell Mr Smith about it. I won't go to sleep. I must talk to Mr Smith. We *must* find the Unicorn. I must stay awake.' But he couldn't.

A short, sharp noise woke him. It took him a while to remember where he was, and why he felt he shouldn't be there. He lay still, trying to decide what had made him wake up. The noise came again. It was the sound of a stone hitting a pane in the window. He put on his glasses, and tiptoed across the room to peep out around the half-drawn curtain. Mr Smith was standing on the starlit terrace, looking up at him. He put his fingers to his lips, then said, quietly but clearly: 'Fetch Fred. Get dressed, both of you, and come out, quickly.'

Simon did as he was told, and, soon, they were

both creeping downstairs and letting themselves out through the back door. Bedwyr, with one eye still half shut, crept after them.

'I meant to stay awake.' Simon said to Mr Smith. 'The Unicorn still isn't safe, is it?'

'No. We can't leave it on the mountain. It won't be safe there. Pettigrew hasn't given up yet.'

'Simon said he hadn't,' Fred said. 'He was sure that he was still looking for it.'

'Is he up there, looking now?' Simon asked.

'Not at the moment, but he has been here looking for something. I hid in the lane, and watched for him, you see. He has searched every corner of the garden, the shed and the terrace, and made a very good attempt at burgling your house.

'Does he think we brought the Unicorn indoors with us?' Fred said.

'No. He was looking for the horn,' Simon told them.

'What makes you think that?' Mr Smith asked.

'Because it still feels odd when I hold it, and I think it still has some use. Perhaps he's read a lot about it in the Historian, and he *knows* that it's still useful.'

'Useful for what?' Fred asked. 'What other use could it have? Do you think there's another Unicorn waiting to be found?'

'Ah! That's it!' Mr Smith said. 'But it wouldn't be a different Unicorn waiting to be found. There is never more than one Unicorn on Earth at one time. But perhaps the horn can still be used to find this one, wherever it may be.'

'I'll fetch it,' Simon said. 'I put it under my

112

pillow.'

He hurried back up to his room, feeling very excited and just a little nervous. What would it feel like this time? Would he see a blue light? Would there be another big flash of lightning? The horn felt almost alive. He was afraid it would work before he reached Mr Smith and Fred. He didn't want to be alone when it happened. He might not be able to stop it withoutFred there to take it away from him. He almost ran downstairs, and burst out through the back door.

A hand reached out from nowhere, and pulled him down into the shadows. Another hand was pressed across his mouth before he could scream.

'Sorry, Simon.' Mr Smith whispered in his ear. 'I had to stop you making a noise. Pettigrew and Bowcett are in the lane. Stay here quietly, while I see what they're doing.'

Simon crouched, almost afraid to breathe. He sat on his hands. He must keep them well away from the horn. It mustn't begin to work while Pettigrew was near. He wondered where Fred was. He hoped Bedwyr would keep quiet.

After what seemed to be an age, Mr Smith appeared beside him, and beckoned him to follow. They crept through the garden to the shed, where Fred was crouching with Bedwyr. She was terribly worried.

'Smithy what are we going to do?' she wailed. 'He's got a gun! I saw it! A horrible, long, black shotgun. He's going to shoot the Unicorn!'

'Now, Fred, keep calm, and don't talk so loudly,' Mr Smith said. 'We have the horn. We can find it before they do. Now, Simon. Let's see what you can do.'

Simon took hold of the horn with both hands and grasped it firmly. At once, he felt the power begin to work. The horn swung around like a hand on a magnetic compass. He didn't try to fight it this time. There were no jerks or sharp movements, just one, smooth, steady swing. It stopped with the sharp end pointing straight at the top of the mountain. They all looked.

'Can you see anything. Is there a blue light?' Fred asked.

'I can see nothing, nothing but darkness,' Mr Smith said.

Simon smiled. He could see the Unicorn, gleaming white among the grey stones of the carn. As he looked at it, it glanced up, and he was sure that it looked straight back at him.

'It's right at the top,' he said. 'I think it knows I've found it. Perhaps it will stay there until I come again.'

Mr Smith took the horn and handed it to Fred.

'Right! We'll have to hurry. They're in front of us, remember, but they won't know your secret path, Fred. You take Simon that way, and I'll follow them along the usual track. I'll stick to Pettigrew like a shadow. Then if he does find the Unicorn first, I can stop him hurting it. But there should be no need for that. You should reach it first. You must try to catch it and, somehow, lead it away.'

'Where shall we take it?' Fred asked.

He thought for a moment. 'Take it home, to Ty

Corn Du. It ought to know that place. It might even go there of its own accord.'

He left them and disappeared into the darkness along the path which led to the blue stone and the hole. Fred took Simon along the path in the opposite direction for a few yards, then turned off it on to a very narrow sheep-track which seemed to lead straight up the mountain side with no bends or twists in it at all. It was very steep, and she almost ran. Simon stumbled along behind her, determined to keep up.

They saw no sign of Pettigrew or Billy, nor of Mr Smith. The only noises on the mountain were the usual ones of sheep and owls. Simon wished that he could stop and hold the horn again and take another look to see if the Unicorn was still there.

'It must wait! It must wait!' he thought.

At the foot of the carn, Fred waited for him.

'We're just in time,' she said. 'It's not nearly as dark as it was. We'll only just manage to get it home before daylight.' She turned around and peered up at the mass of grey rocks rising steeply above them. 'There's something white up there. It must be it. Come on!' They scrambled from rock to rock, straight up, ignoring the track.

The Unicorn was standing in a small, flat patch of wiry grass, surrounded by huge, grey, lichen-covered boulders. It was calm and un-worried, and quite unaware of any danger, as it held its beautiful head high, and gazed out towards the sea.

'Better leave it to me,' Fred said. 'Only girls can catch them, remember.' She put down the horn.

Simon said nothing, but stood quietly at the
edge of the grass patch, watching her as she walked
towards it, slowly, with her hand outstretched.
The Unicorn turned and looked at her. It tossed its
head a little, and its white mane spread like a fine
cloud of gossamer above its delicately arched neck.
It stood still and let her stroke its nose and rest her
hand gently on its shoulder. Then it bent its head
and sniffed at Bedwyr who had followed at her
heels.

'How is she going to lead it away?' Simon thought. 'She'll have to hold on to its mane. I hope she can do it. She'll have to be quick. I'd better be ready to follow them. I mustn't leave the horn behind.' He picked it up.

The Unicorn raised its head proudly, and looked at him. He could see it quite clearly. It had the same look in its eyes. It gave one joyful bell-like call of welcome, and walked across the grass towards him. He held out his hand, expecting it to come to be stroked.

But, when it reached the place where he stood waiting, the Unicorn stopped. Then, very gracefully, and with great dignity, it knelt before him, and pressed the point of its long, black horn into the ground at his feet.

14 *Last Encounter with Billy*

They didn't have to make the Unicorn come with them, or even to lead it. It was quite content to follow Simon wherever he went. It stood beside him, and they gazed out at the Islands together for a moment. The castle was as bright as a Christmas tree.

'That was what it was looking at when we found it,' Simon thought. He wasn't at all surprised that the Unicorn could see it. It seemed only natural that it should be able to.

Quickly, he followed Fred and Bedwyr down another very narrow sheep-track, through the rough boulders and huge tufts of coarse, wiry heather. He was a little afraid that the Unicorn might stumble and hurt itself, but it picked its way as nimbly as a goat. Fred waited at the foot of the carn again.

'We'll take the wide, main path,' she said. 'We'll be able to run faster on that.'

'We might meet Pettigrew that way.'

'We might, but, if we do Smithy will be right behind him, and, anyway, the Unicorn will take care of him.'

Simon remembered the way the Unicorn had charged. He didn't want that to happen again. It might not miss a second time. He also remembered Pettigrew's gun.

'I'll stand in front of it all the time,' he thought. 'Then Pettigrew won't dare shoot . . . will he?'

They set off rapidly, with Fred and Bedwyr in the lead. It was still fairly dark, a sort of dim, grey darkness, and Simon couldn't quite see the path, but he kept up with Fred and hoped that he wouldn't trip or stumble. He could hear the Unicorn cantering along lightly behind him. They soon reached the dark hole with the huge, tipped-up stone. The Unicorn snorted with distaste as it hurried past.

'It's never going to be shut up anywhere, ever again,' Simon vowed. 'We'll take it somewhere where it's safe for it to be free. Where will it be safe?' He hoped that Mr Smith would know of somewhere.

Suddenly, Fred stopped. Simon blundered into her, and peered past her shoulder. A big, dark figure loomed up out of the gloom.

'It's Bowcett,' Fred whispered. 'He's seen us. He's coming!' She was panicking. He could hear it in her voice.

Quite calmly, he handed her the horn, and pushed past her to stand in front. He knew that this was one fight he would have to win, and, for the first time in his life, he wasn't afraid of Billy Bowcett. It didn't seem to matter if he finished this fight hurt. He wasn't worried about himself any more. The only important thing was that the Unicorn must be saved. In fact, he felt very annoyed that Billy should be getting in his way.

'Jonesy, Jonesy, Jonesy! Out in the dark! I'll have to call you Owl Eyes in future, not Four Eyes, won't I!' Billy stood, squarely, feet apart, in the middle of the path.

'Get out of the way, Billy,' Simon said. 'You're blocking the path.'

'Want to run home, do you? What's the hurry? Pinched something, have you? Someone out to get you?' Bedwyr began to growl. Billy peered past Simon's legs. 'Keep that mangey brute off me, or Pettigrew'll shoot it.'

'Hold on to him, Fred,' Simon said quietly. He could feel the Unicorn pressing against his shoulder. It wanted to get past him. He heard it pawing and stamping on the ground as it had before it charged at Pettigrew. He leant against it, trying to keep it back. 'You're going to have to get out of the way, Billy,' he said.

Billy was surprised. He gave a short, nervous laugh. 'Have to! What's all this? Jonesy giving orders!' His voice was just a little too loud.

'He's worried,' Simon thought. 'He can't believe it's me, not afraid of him.' He began to feel excited. 'You're going to have to get out of the way,' he repeated.

'Who's going to make me?' Billy asked.

'I am,' Simon said.

At that moment, the Unicorn gave him a gentle, but firm, push. He almost fell forward, but saved himself by stepping right up in front of Billy. Billy stepped backwards, then stopped and raised his fists.

'Speed!' Simon thought. 'Be quick! Grab him!'

He reached out for his arm, and missed. Billy had stepped backwards again. He was staring past him, over his shoulder. Staring at something he had just noticed.

'What's that on that donkey's head?' he asked. Then he sniggered. 'Oh, it's Pettigrew's horn, tied on. Thought you'd hide it that way, did you. Trust you to think of something clever-clever.'

The Unicorn stamped its cloven hooves again, and tossing its head, gave one, great, bell-like call. Then it charged. Simon threw himself at Billy and pushed him out of the way. They landed in a heap in the heather, and the Unicorn leapt past, and galloped head-long, down the path, and away towards the awakening village. With a little worried cry, Fred leapt after it, and sped like the wind with Bedwyr at her heels.

15 *Mr Smith and the Wheelbarrow*

Simon felt quite dazed. It had all happened so quickly. He staggered to his feet and began to run after them. 'Don't lose it, Fred!' he called, then wished he hadn't, for someone was running down the path behind him. 'It's Pettigrew! He heard me shout! He's coming!' He headed for the cottage gateway, dived through, and slammed the gate shut behind him. It was dark there. A big rhododendron hid him from the path. He stood and watched.

It wasn't only Pettigrew who was running down the path. It was Billy too. But they weren't chasing him. Pettigrew was chasing Billy. And as Simon watched, he caught him. Somehow, he got hold of Billy's right arm, and twisted it behind his back, and then he hit him, hard, on the side of his head. He didn't shout at him. He spoke in a low voice, making each syllable as sharp and clear as ice, and to emphasize some words he twisted Billy's arm just a little more.

'You let it get away. You stupid nincompoop!' he said.

Billy winced with pain. 'You didn't tell me. I didn't know about it. It attacked me,' he began to whine.

'Shut up! You are an idiot! Do you hear? You are an idiot! A soft-centred, bungling idiot!' He brought his knee up into Billy's back, and hit him again, making him cry out with pain. 'Shut up, you stupid idiot, before I really hurt you,' Billy cried all the more, and tried to squirm away. Pettigrew let go his arm, but caught him by the shoulder and swung him around. Then he clenched his fist, ready to swing a hard punch into Billy's face.

Suddenly, a third figure joined the two on the path. It rose from the heather, swiftly and silently, like a genie coming out of nowhere. Pettigrew spun, lifted, flew through the air, and landed on his back with a thud.

'Mr Smith!' Simon thought, with great satisfaction.

'Get out of the way, young Bowcett,' Mr Smith said calmly, and Simon opened the gate and called to him.

'Billy! Come in here.'

'Now, Smithy,' Pettigrew said, and Simon could tell that he was frightened. 'Let's be reasonable, Smithy. The ruby will be big enough for both of us. Fifty fifty. You and I. How about it?'

'No way, Pettigrew! No way!' Mr Smith said, and then Pettigrew tried to hit him.

Simon and Billy stood side by side and watched. Pettigrew attacked three times. The second time he tried to use the gun as a club, but Mr Smith snatched it from his hand and flung it away. It landed just outside the gate, and Simon crept out and picked it up, taking care to keep out of the way.

Pettigrew's third attack was a wild, headlong

charge. Simon thought that Mr Smith would be knocked over, but he wasn't. He seemed to catch Pettigrew in mid air, flip him over, upside down, and then send him on his way with a deft and powerful movement of his shoulders. Pettigrew landed with an earth-shaking thud, and lay, gasping for breath, in the heather.

Then Mr Smith walked over and took the gun from Simon, and broke it in half over his knee, scattering the cartridges as far as he could throw them.

'A gun to catch a Unicorn! Really Pettigrew!' he said. 'You can never take a Unicorn by force. Never! You really should do your homework properly.'

He took a good look at Billy. 'This should teach you to choose your friends more carefully,' he said. 'Oh dear, this shoulder is quite nasty. If I were you I should hurry along home. If Pettigrew is as fit as he used to be, he'll have recovered fully in about ten minutes, and you don't want to be here then, do you.'

Billy started to shake his head, and winced with pain. He gave Simon one last despairing look, then turned and slunk away as quickly as he could.

'Now,' Mr Smith said, briskly. 'Tell me what happened while I collect my barrow. I took the liberty of hiding it under your rhododendron.'

It was a most odd-looking vehicle. Simon couldn't see it very well in the dim light, but it seemed to be a bamboo basket with two big wheels, a tall mast, and two, long straight poles at one end, like handles.

'We must catch up with them quickly,' Mr Smith said, when he heard how the Unicorn and Fred had raced away. 'Will you sit on, or run beside?'

'Run beside, thank you,' Simon said. He thought the wheelbarrow didn't look safe enough to ride in.

'Right,' Mr Smith said. 'But hold on tightly to the side. It picks up speed very quickly.'

He hoisted a square, brown sail, and they set off at a fantastic rate along the mountain path, through the village and out on to the sands. A huge flock of birds rose noisily as they disturbed their roosting, and the cows on the hill all panicked and charged around with tails in the air. The wheelbarrow lifted Simon off his feet with each step he took. He felt as though he was almost flying with the birds, charging with the cows. Their noise and clamour filled the air all around him, and all was confusion.

But when they reached the gateway to the beech avenue, they seemed to enter a wonderful silence.

'Slow down! Slow down!' Simon's voice was a hoarse whisper. He felt he mustn't shout. He mustn't disturb the peace. Something was happening there. 'It sounds . . . no, it looks different,' he said. 'It's all sort of grey and misty.'

Mr Smith stopped the barrow. They took down the sail, and walked forward slowly. The wheels of the barrow just fitted across the strip of poppies. Simon was glad about that. He looked up at the canopy of leaves. They hung motionless. There was no wind. Everything was still and quiet.

'Listen!' he said, and pulled at Mr Smith's arm. 'There's no noise. No noise at all. It's as though everything is listening, or watching, even the poppies.'

A small, white shape came bounding to meet them. It was Bedwyr. He jumped up at Mr Smith, wagging his tail, then scampered off again, back towards the house. Suddenly, Mr Smith gasped, and gripped Simon by the arm.

'It's the Unicorn!' he whispered. 'It's here, in the avenue with Fred and Meryl.'

Simon could only see a white blur in the shadows of the tall trees.

'I must go closer,' he said.

'We might frighten it. We had better stay here.'

'It won't be frightened of me.'

'But it might not like me.'

'Oh, it won't mind you. You're my friend.'

Mr Smith said no more. Simon could feel him, tense and excited, beside him as they walked forward very slowly.

Meryl was draped in a long, white shawl. Her eyes were like big, dark pools in her pale face. She was standing, with her arm around Fred as she stroked the beautiful creature just as she had done on the carn. They both glanced up when they saw Simon and Mr Smith.

The Unicorn turned its head quickly. It leapt around to face them. For a moment, it stood exactly as it had in the ice . . . alert and poised, ready for flight. Simon stood still. Slowly the Unicorn relaxed. It lowered its foreleg, and stood with its head high, scenting the air. Then it bent its neck and shook out its mane like a white cloud. It pawed at the ground seven times, then, with a whisk of its curling tail, it trotted towards him, calling softly, just one, mellow chime, and knelt, once again, at his feet.

16 A Home for the Unicorn

'It does that every time it meets you,' Fred said. 'It pays homage, as though you were a king.'

'Or a new, great wizard,' Mr Smith said softly. 'How it loves you, Simon! It looks at you as though it would follow you to the end of the earth.' Meryl was standing very still, simply looking at the Unicorn. He went across and put his arm around her.

'Where did it come from, Smithy?' she said. 'Does it belong to Simon?'

'No, my love,' he said. 'A Unicorn never belongs to anybody . . . but it is Simon's friend.' He told her all about it as they walked to the Summer House.

There, they sat and talked about what to do next.

'We have to find somewhere safe for it to live,' Simon said.

'It could live here, in our garden, couldn't it, Meryl?' Fred said. 'It's very quiet here, we're never bothered by Oysters.'

'Pettigrew comes here,' Meryl reminded her.

'And it wouldn't be free, cooped up in a garden, even a nice one like this,' Simon said, standing with his cheek against the Unicorn's soft, smooth neck.

'We're not going to be able to give it real freedom, Simon,' Mr Smith said.

'But we must!' Simon was determined. 'It wants to be free. It must never be shut up anywhere, ever again. Isn't there anywhere really wild where we could take it to live?'

'I can think of nowhere.' Mr Smith sounded sad. 'Not even Tregarron Bog would be wild and safe enough to contain it.'

'Somewhere in Scotland, maybe,' Fred suggested. 'Where there are Ospreys and Eagles and Red Deer. Somewhere in the Hebrides.'

Mr Smith shook his head. 'It would still be in danger, I feel, even in the most remote Hebridean Island.'

'Island!' Suddenly, Simon knew where the Unicorn could live in peace. 'There *are* Islands where it will be safe,' he said. 'It was looking at them when we found it on top of the carn. We must take it to the Golden Islands in the mist. It's the only place where it can be really free.'

Meryl didn't think that Fred should go there if the Islands were invisible to her, and Fred didn't like the idea either. It frightened her. But she insisted on going with them. Simon thought that she was very brave. He knew what it felt like to be faced with something you couldn't see.

It was Fred who suggested borrowing the old, flat-bottomed punt. She knew where the boys kept it. She even knew where they hid the oars. They fixed the wheelbarrow sail into a hole in the stern, which was really meant for a tiller, then, with Fred, wrapped in Meryl's white shawl, sitting cuddling Bedwyr on the seat below the sail, Mr Smith rowing from amidships, and Simon crouching in the bows with the Unicorn lying at his feet, they set out down the river to the sea.

Meryl watched them go, then turned away, and began to walk quickly towards the village. Simon could see her, a pale blur, moving across the bridge. She was going to the cottage to wake Mother and Dad, and tell them where he had gone.

'Mother might be surprised,' he thought, 'but Dad won't be.' He rested his hand on the Unicorn's shoulder. He wished that Dad could have seen it, but there hadn't been time. They had been afraid to wait. Mr Smith hadn't said so, but Simon guessed that he was still worried about Pettigrew. Yes. They couldn't wait. They had to be quick.

But, after the speed of the wheelbarrow, their progress seemed painfully slow. Mr Smith rowed well, but Simon could see that, even with the river current and the tide helping them, it would take hours to reach the Islands. He began to worry. It was no longer dark, the cold, clear light of dawn had driven away the mist and the safe, grey shadows. The village was almost awake. He could hear a radio in the camp site near the estuary, and the sound of voices carried clearly across the water from the dinghy beach. Someone was going sailing early.

He listened to the scrape of a keel on shingle, then the splashing as the boat reached the first small waves on the shore. There was the cough of an engine being started. Then silence. Then another cough, and another. Then the engine burst into life with a spluttering roar. Next moment it had settled down to a purposeful chug. He had heard that sound before.

'That's Pettigrew's outboard motor! It is! I know it is!' Fred rocked the punt as she turned, frantically, to catch the harbour entrance.

'Steady, Fred! Steady!' Mr Smith tried to calm her, but he couldn't.

'Row faster!' she screamed. 'Row faster! He'll catch us!'

'You're not thinking,' he told her. 'How can an old punt, rowed by one man, escape from a fast dinghy with an outboard motor? We can't, can we? We haven't the same power.'

'But we have got power!' Simon thought. 'I have. And so has the horn. Fred!' he said. 'Where's the horn?'

Mr Smith looked at him intently. 'What have you in mind?' he asked.

'We need more power, you said. Well, maybe . . . the horn . . . if I hold it.'

Mr Smith reached forward and took the horn from beneath Fred's seat. 'The key to all our problems,' he said, and handed it to Simon. 'Go ahead! Quickly!'

Simon held the horn with both hands. It still felt warm and alive. But it didn't move. It didn't throb or twist. It just lay still.

'It's not working any more. It's not moving at all.' He almost cried with despair.

'Try doing something with it. Point it at something. Touch the Unicorn's horn with it.'

The Unicorn was watching every move Simon made. It didn't like being touched with the horn. It tossed its head as he brought it close, and jerked away sharply.

'Sorry!' Simon said. 'Steady now.' He reached out quickly to calm it.

The moment his left hand touched the Unicorn's neck, the horn in his right hand began to tremble. The Unicorn lay still again, but the black horn shivered. Faster and faster it went, with small, quick movements which made his whole arm shake. And, as it vibrated, it began to hum.

The hum was very quiet at first, but, as the movement of the horn quickened, the hum grew louder and climbed to a higher note. Higher and higher it climbed until it became a clear, almost warbling whistle. It seemed as though every other noise around them was frozen into silence. Even the waves stopped lapping and splashing against the punt. The sea lay as flat and calm as a mirror. Only Pettigrew's engine throbbed, nearer and nearer.

Then, a terrific gust of wind hit them. It pinned their arms to their sides and pressed against them with such force that they could hardly breathe. The punt was held absolutely still in its grasp. Simon felt as though he would never be able to move again. He tried to gasp for breath. He couldn't even open his mouth. He heard Pettigrew's motor splutter and falter. Then it stopped . . . And nothing could be heard but the sound of

134

churning, boiling waves.

Just as suddenly as it came, the gale went . . . and a warm, gentle breeze began to blow. Simon sniffed. He could smell the sweet, heavy, almost sickly scent of flowers.

'Rhododendrons!' he said.

'And pine trees,' said Mr Smith.

'And roast chestnuts.'

'And mulled wine.'

'And honey and milk.'

'What is it? What is it?' Fred looked terrified.

'It's a wind sent from the Islands, sent to carry us safely,' Mr Smith told her. He shipped the oars and moved across to sit beside her. 'Right!' he called across the water. 'We're ready!'

Simon felt the breeze like fingers in his hair. The Unicorn's mane lifted and blew against his face. He saw the edge of Fred's shawl rise a little, and Mr Smith's baggy trousers flapped against his legs. Then the wind moved around behind them. It filled the square, brown, sail, and sent the little craft skimming over the white-capped waves towards the Golden Islands. Simon moved a little nearer to the Unicorn, and leant against its strong, hard shoulder. It raised its head, and blew, gently, through its soft nostrils. It was a warm and friendly noise.

'Now it will be safe and free,' he thought. He felt warm and comfortable inside, simply thinking about it.

But Fred still looked uneasy. 'I wish I could see where we were going,' she kept saying. 'I wish I could see them.' Mr Smith put his arm around her to comfort her. Simon did so wish that she could share it with them. There were gnarled trees alive with golden butterflies, beetles as black as ebony, and gnats like diamonds hanging on the air beneath the branches. He could see every detail of them all. He could see the steep island, too, with the castle perched on top of it. It was like a glittering jewel set in the deep blue sea. Lights still shone from every one of its tall, narrow windows. He could hear the music of harps and flutes and violins, and singing and laughter. 'And Fred can't see it,' he thought. 'I wish she could. I wonder if I could *do* something to help her see it all. I must think of something.'

'Look, Simon!' Mr Smith said. 'Someone is coming to meet us.'

A flight of wide, white steps led down from the golden castle, past the glittering cliff to a narrow, stone jetty which jutted out into the sea. At the foot of the steps stood a woman with a golden crown upon her head. Her dress shimmered like dragonflies' wings as she came stepping towards them so lightly that she seemed to be floating. She drifted to the very edge of the jetty, and there, she waited.

The punt sailed along-side, then hove-to some distance from the rough, stone wall. Simon looked up at her. She was smiling down at him, a strange, half-smile, with her eyes almost serious but kind and happy. She said nothing, but nodded to him as though he was a long-expected visitor. The Unicorn looked up at her, and called softly and she raised one thin, white arm, and pointed to the next island, the island of steep, golden cliffs and pine

trees. The punt slid forward again.

Simon looked back at the woman as they sailed away. She was still pointing, and the shimmering sleeve of her dress floated away from her arm like a delicate, fluttering wing. The Unicorn was watching her too. It raised its head and called again. Simon glanced down at it for an instant, and when he looked back again, she had gone.

They passed beneath the rainbow, and sailed up to a wide stretch of golden sand at the foot of the sheer cliff. Dense banks of rhododendrons stretched away on either side. The scent of their flowers hung heavily on the air. The Unicorn stood up. Simon crouched against the gunwale to make room for it.

They swept across the wide bay and headed for the very centre of the beach. The flat bottom of the punt scraped gently as it slid through shallow rippling wavelets, up on to the golden shore. The Unicorn stood still for one moment, looking down at Simon. Then it bent its graceful neck and nudged him gently on the forehead with its soft, white nose. Next moment, it leapt lightly over the bow on to the sand.

Quickly, Simon jumped after it. This was the chance he had been waiting for. The chance to help Fred see the island. It would be his only chance. If he could just touch the beach for one second, she would see it. He held tightly to the gunwale with his left hand, and reached down with his right hand. Already the punt was drifting out. It pulled him away, back into the sea. He stretched his arm and groped through the wavelets. His fingers touched the sand, just for one brief moment.

'Oh!' Fred cried out with joy. 'I saw it! I saw it!' Mr Smith caught him under his arms and lifted him, wet and dripping, back into the boat, and they both crouched in the bows, looking back at the Unicorn.

It stood, proud and magnificent, on the golden beach. Across the water, distantly, they heard its voice ring out, one last time. Then it whirled around and kicked up its heels, and sped away towards the pine-covered cleft in the hills . . . wild and free.

17 *The New Wizard?*

Simon knelt in the bows of the punt with the horn cradled in his arms, and watched the mountain rushing to meet them as the island breeze carried them back to the shore. He felt happy and contented.

Fred couldn't stop talking about the things he had helped her to see. She was still talking as they swept into the estuary, where Dad and Mother were waiting with Meryl. Dad could smell the scent of the islands on the breeze, and Fred began at the beginning again, and told him all about everything, as they stowed away the punt and hid the oars and climbed into the car to drive to Ty Corn Du.

Mother was very quiet while Fred was talking, and as Mr Smith told them all about the Unicorn, she sat in a corner of Meryl's kitchen looking lost and bewildered.

'But why did the Unicorn kneel to Simon?' she asked. 'It was paying homage, wasn't it, but Simon's not a king. He's just an ordinary little boy.'

'Ah no!' Mr Smith said. 'If I may dare to contradict, after knowing him for such a short time.

Simon is not an ordinary little boy. He has the capacity to be a very Superior Person.'

'What on earth do you mean?' Mother asked.

'In China,' Mr Smith explained, 'there are Unicorn legends, just as there are in Britain, but they are not like British legends, nor indeed, like most Unicorn legends throughout the world. The Chinese Unicorn is called Ki-lin. It has nothing to do with rubies or poison, and no-one ever wants to catch it for their own use. It simply exists as a Most Superior, special animal ... but ... it only appears at the coming of a great man. It is said that one appeared at the birth of Confucius.'

Fred began to jump around. 'I know what Simon is! He's the great dyn hysbys in all our stories. The one who will one day come to live in Ty Corn Du. Only he's come to Ty Corn Du Fach instead, and the Unicorn marked him coming *here* where he belongs instead of when he was in London.'

Simon wished they wouldn't talk about him. He cradled the horn in his arms again, and hoped that someone would change the subject. They did for a while.

Somehow they started talking about belonging, and Dad said that he never, ever, wanted to move away from the mountain. Simon heard him say that he was getting better, that the specialist at the hospital had said that there was no reason why he shouldn't live to a ripe old age as long as he lived a quiet life. Then Mother and Mr Smith and Meryl joined in, and, in no time at all, they had planned that Dad would buy a boat and give sailing lessons

141

to the Oysters, and Mother would be a landscape gardener, and get people to pay her for creating beautiful gardens for them. Then Meryl, rather shyly, told them that she and Mr Smith were going to be married, and live at Ty Corn Du together, and keep Fred with them, always. Simon saw Fred hide her face in Bedwyr to stop everyone seeing her crying with happiness.

But it wasn't long before they began to talk about him again.

'All I wish,' Dad said, 'is that Mam-gu was still alive, so that I could tell her that Simon has "the hands".' Everyone looked at Simon.

'You see!' Fred said. 'He fulfils that legend, too! He *is* a dyn hysbys.'

'Yes!' Meryl said. 'I shall fix the black horn back up in its place on the wall, Simon. It will be there any time you need it.'

Simon looked at Mother. She said nothing. She simply sat and stared, and listened as Mr Smith talked of mathematics and philosophy, until the door bell rang and interrupted him. Fred ran to answer it. She was soon back . . . and she was carrying the Myddfai Historian.

She dumped it on the table in front of Simon. 'That was Bowcett!' she said. 'He wouldn't come in. He just left this for Simon. Do you know, that wretched Pettigrew didn't drown after all! He swam ashore, but he's bolted now, gone for good, I hope. Bowcett said his father stopped Pettigrew taking this, but *he* doesn't want it. I gathered that he never wants to see either the book or Pettigrew again. It's all too weird for him. Do you know what he said . . . Pettigrew lost his dark glasses in that squall, so they could see his eyes, at last, and do you know what! He hasn't got any eye lids! Just eyes, wide open, always.' She shuddered. 'Anyway, Bowcett says that Jonesy's the one who's friends with the Unicorn, so Jonesy had better have the book about it . . . Jonesy!' she said. 'If there's one thing worse than a witch called Fred, it's a wizard called Jonesy!'

Simon had had enough. Even Billy was treating him like a wizard now.

'You've got it all wrong!' he said. 'All of you. The important thing is the Unicorn, not me. It only knelt because it liked me, because I found it and set it free. It was only saying thank you. It's the Unicorn which is wonderful. I'm not going to be great at all.'

Mr Smith smiled, and his eyes closed into slanting, narrow slits. 'I wonder,' he said. 'I wonder.'

Also available from Knight Books

ELIZABETH GOUDGE

☐ 02427 5   Linnets and Valerians   £1.25

NICHOLAS FISK

☐ 24878 5   Starstormers   £1.50
☐ 24879 3   Sunburst   £1.50
☐ 26529 9   Catfang   £1.50
☐ 27076 4   Evil Eye   £1.50
☐ 32093 1   Volcano   £1.50

All these books are available at your local bookshop or newsagent, or can be ordered direct from the publisher. Just tick the titles you want and fill in the form below.

Prices and availability subject to change without notice.

KNIGHT BOOKS, P.O. Box 11, Falmouth, Cornwall.

Please send cheque or postal order, and allow the following for postage and packing:

U.K. – 55p for one book, plus 22p for the second book, and 14p for each additional book ordered up to a £1.75 maximum.

B.F.P.O. and EIRE – 55p for the first book, plus 22p for the second book, and 14p per copy for the next 7 books, 8p per book thereafter.

OTHER OVERSEAS CUSTOMERS – £1.00 for the first book, plus 25p per copy for each additional book.

Name ....

Address ....

....